PASSION PATROL SERIES

COMBAT

By

Emma Calin

*Previously published as 'Knockout!',
'Passion Patrol 1' and 'Seduction of Combat'*

Published 2019
by Gallo-Romano Media

© Emma Calin 2019

ISBN-13: 9781916441163
Combat

www.gallo-romano.co.uk

Previously published © Emma Calin 2017

ISBN-13: 978999913212
Seduction of Combat

Previously published © Emma Calin 2012

ISBN-13:978-1463630904

ISBN-10: 1463630905
Knockout!

To: Nicola, Jo, Dave, Kate, Matt, Will, Izzy

Prologue

Promotion had put her back in uniform. It felt good to be behind the wheel of a marked police vehicle, slowly cruising the London streets. All afternoon she'd been jargon juggling. Finally she'd escaped and taken advantage of a spare emergency response car to drive to the adjoining area for a conference on community initiatives.

She clicked on the radio. This was how her earlier career had been, among the run-down fast food shops, the loitering drivers smoking weed outside the mini cab offices, the boom of music from cars and buildings, the glitzy bill boards in the heart of dilapidation. Suddenly an urgent voice calling Met' Police control at Scotland Yard.

"Lima Three... Lima Three to MP... we have a fail to stop... high speed North towards the city."

She caught the familiar sound of a chase. A vehicle was fleeing a patrol car about two miles behind her and coming her way. She pulled over and listened. She need not be involved in this. This was not her job. So she'd been top student at the Hendon driving school of the Metropolitan Police. She was an Inspector now and this was not about ego or drama. She knew that. She knew that!

She checked out the siren and blue light controls. The big V8 engine rumbled playfully. She blipped the throttle and felt the tight knot of its unexpressed power. It had started to rain. And this was not her job!

"Eighty, that's eight zero miles per hour. Driver looks about 15 years old... running red light into Brixton now... wait... wait... straight through... still at eighty."

Her heart rate increased. These would be crowded streets in the late afternoon. Now only a mile behind her the chase was closing in. She absorbed the details. The target car was a stolen boy racer Ford. At least four joy riding kids from a delinquent home were desperately trying to escape. Again a more urgent voice...

"We have a tire blowout. We can't continue. Lima Three over..."

She checked the mirror. The target vehicle was approaching still at high speed - reckless speed. It screamed past, taking a traffic island on the wrong side of the road. She caught the eye of a shaven headed boy in the back seat as she hit the lights and sirens and slammed down the throttle.

"Lima Delta One... in pursuit," she announced.

Soon she was right on the tail. She had more power and more skill. They barreled into the Camberwell New Road junction at seventy miles per hour. The target car side-swiped a red London bus but straightened up. She concentrated hard. The rain was turning the tarmac into a skid pan. She saw more police blue lights ahead near the Oval tube station. The target feinted right then tried to corner left. The tail started to slide out on the wet road. She watched in slow motion as the vehicle slammed into a street lamp. A spray of glass and the scream of tortured metal suddenly gave way to an utter utter silence. An awful stillness enveloped the wreck and nothing moved. Nobody moved. The radio carried the voice of Scotland Yard control...

"Discontinue pursuit. Repeat discontinue. Speed too high for safety. Lima Delta One - acknowledge... discontinue pursuit..."

Combat

A Passion Patrol Series Novel

Chapter 1

Anna Leyton pushed purposefully through the revolving doors. The swish of wheels on the wet London streets, the clack and shuffle of anonymous feet on Victoria Street hardly caught her attention. She looked across at St James's Tube Station, past the constantly turning triangular sign that proclaimed "New Scotland Yard."

Ten years ago the very sight of the tall office block behind her would have filled her with pride. This evening it seemed no more than any other building in London. Even the city itself had lost the charisma that had filled her heart and soul with excitement as a young police recruit at the age of twenty one. Now the great animal which was the city shrugged off its joys and sorrows and ploughed on through time without a care for any flea on its back.

The afternoon had been tough. As a mere Inspector she had been a junior in a room filled with older and more senior men. The days had long gone when they would have asked why she wasn't at home with the babies. All the same, she was a woman in a macho world. Her career was back on track although too damaged to think of the very top. Her personal life - well - she was a cop ok. She had already lived out a decade of her youth at a broken bottle edge of society - where the sharpest cuts had been to herself.

The evening was cold and pitiless. She pulled up the collar of her raincoat, tightening the belt around her slim waist. Rain began to dampen her long dark hair. As an Interpol officer, she had the freedom to wear her hair as she wanted. She cursed not having brought her umbrella. At the same time her mind jangled with the responsibilities of her new assignment. When she had graduated with a degree in modern languages and had turned her back on her family's famous luxury motor-yacht business, her mother had declared that she was about to waste her life. Like her mother was a wasted life expert.

At the entrance to the tube station there was a growing crowd. The lattice shutters were being closed while an harassed official explained that there was a wild-cat strike. She turned away. Ahead of her lay a nightmare journey by bus to her empty flat in Kilburn. Suddenly the cold politics of the meeting, the gray loneliness of the street, the crowds of uncaring strangers, filled her with a longing for warmth and intimacy. The break from her lover, police Commander Beaumont Locke had seemed clean but had left a jagged gap of loneliness - like an exit wound. A gap where another rainy evening briefly played over and over again in her mind.

She stood on the edge of the pavement. Perhaps she could get a taxi - but with a tube strike there was small chance of that! Several black cabs beetled along, already filled. She kept her hand raised and as if by magic she saw the amber "For Hire" light of a London taxi pulling in at her side. She felt a movement from behind and heard an accented male voice:

"Zee 'eelton 'otel, Park Lane."

She turned to see a tall rock of a man, moving past her into the taxi. This guy was going to have to back off. She grabbed the door. Even as she did so she saw his deep brown eyes, the dark eyebrows, one of which only partly disguised a long scar. She could never explain - even to herself - why in that instant she wanted to touch it and know how it had been caused. Her heart raced with indignation and a sense of excitement she had never expected to feel again...not since... well, just not since everything.

"This cab stopped for me!" she snapped.

"Possiblement," growled the stranger, but smiling with slow gentle eyes, a Gallic down-turn of the mouth and a shrug of his wide shoulders.

"We can be - 'ow you say - in the same sheep?"

"I think you mean boat - unless you do mean sheep." she replied, unable to stop herself returning his smile. The accent was pure Clouseau. This guy just had to be some kind of fake. So much fake that any cop would hitch up for a ride just to keep in practice.

The cabbie had already started his meter.

"Anyone gettin' in - there's plenty of takers?"

Anna watched the stranger's face, the thick short cut hair, the tough broad bridge of his nose. His strong hand remained on the door. Gently he brought his other hand around to her back and eased her forward into the cab. She was breathless, as if she had become merely a note in a melody that had always been playing in her head. This could not be her life. OK girl - get real, this is just some arrogant man. Just one more. He regarded her with a look that reached deep into her and stroked a sweet spot in the base of her stomach. She didn't want this… but he was still doing it.

He indicated with his powerful hand that she should sit opposite him. Against all instincts she found herself complying. The cab moved off, nosing out into the London traffic. The wipers tapped rhythmically, the lights from the department stores spilled out melting into the gray flowing river of road and pavement.

"So - yes - we are in the same sheep," he smiled gently, "but I must say 'boat' yes?"

"If you're into sheep it's ok with me," she returned, wondering why she was smiling and feeling a sensation of warmth. Sure - this was some kind of grease but for a few moments it was nice to slide along.

He smiled again, showing even white teeth behind the full wide lips that pouted forward as he spoke in such a way that just possibly he really was French.

Sitting opposite him, she could take in the full presence of this stranger. It was as if he transmitted a force - an aura of danger and a sardonic humorous innocence. She attempted to re-assert her normal senses - her ability to appraise a man, threat or situation in the blink of an eye - a skill she had honed on the streets of South London - in a world of gangs, drugs and murder. And yet - here she was, tripping over the bags that some stupid girl had left in the entrance to her brain.

"Luckily Park Lane is on the way to Kilburn," she said with deliberate plainness.

He looked back at her, holding her eyes, then making a slow upward sweep of her whole body, like a lick of cool flame that swept through the centre line of her thighs, her belly, her breasts. He shrugged.

"It would not matter Madame - I would be your knight in sighing armor."

Anna shook her head in disbelief at his clumsy deliberate mistake and glanced quickly at his smiling brown eyes. This guy was larger than two lives. This was pure panto.

"You laugh at a poor little French boy?"

"Not laugh - you just kinda trowel it on don't you?"

"OK - you got me," he drawled in relaxed Californian,"you're a cop right. Outside Scotland Yard - you must think I'm pretty dumb."

She scrambled for grip. This was a moment - a turning point. Why could she not, at least for a few delicious minutes, be Anna Leyton, service number - zero, rank - woman of this Earth, no police record, no medals, no blood?

"A cop - for God's sake - do I look like a cop?" she spat at him - hoping he would accept the question as a denial. Any detective knew that a suspect answering a question with a question is beginning to struggle. He nodded seriously.

"Please forgive - I mustn't tease! So, anyhow, what do you do?"

"I sell boats," she stated plainly. Tie a truth to a lie - you can even believe it yourself.

"Ah yes - the London rain is very famous - did you sell a boat today?"

"Yeah - I sold two arks to a Jewish guy with four elephants."

He threw back his head with a deep genuine laugh. She was on top now. She'd follow through the advantage.

"Have you heard of Leyton Marine Sports Yachts?"

"Of course - I saw your new models at the Cannes Boat Show last year - The Nereus 74." Bingo! She knew this model inside out.

"That's top of the range. Evidently you didn't buy?"

"I just did - if you can close the deal."

She smiled at his smoothness. He was deceiving her, she was sure of that. She was paying him back in kind. But just for a few minutes she had been free. She was out and away in a world without flashback - running in childhood meadows, not running from - just running free.

The cab pushed and swished on towards Buckingham Palace. She saw him studying the famous landmark, as if he were checking out the architecture. In profile his face looked even more male - handsome yet warm - the scar above his right eye constantly attracting her gaze. He was a brute of some kind but he could lie even with his eyes. Once again she found herself responding to him and wanting to touch that scar. In this new world of a few out of reality moments with a gorgeous stranger she could let go, becoming aware of the pulse of life in her breasts and a sense of warmth and longing deep in her stomach. She bit her lip as she consciously allowed these feelings to sweep over her. She took in his striped linen jacket, dark trousers and hand stitched leather shoes. His crisp white shirt accentuated the tanned olive tone of his skin. His shoulders were broad with hard muscular upper arms while his beautifully cut clothes proclaimed the body of an athlete or sportsman.

"So, you know what I do. Do you work in London?" she asked wondering if he would tell her the truth - since she had not!

"Oh not at all - I am here to sign some papers that's all."

"Papers?" she questioned too quickly, aware she could be exposing her cover.

"Just a contract - you know, boring business stuff."

He looked at her with a caress in his brown eyes. The cab was at

Hyde Park Corner, just a short way from the Hilton. Her heart hammered. Soon he would step out into the night and never see her again. It had to be that way. You could dream but your story was your story. Better just accept and live it out any way you could.

"You have to sell boats tonight?"

"No... but..."

"So sell me one over a drink at my hotel!" he urged leaning forward, "Surely you want to close on a deal like this?"

She tried to pull herself together. This was fantasy trash with an impossible guy - but what was she afraid of? She could handle this smooth operator, maybe even rough him up a bit.

"But I - I don't have any brochures with me..."

"Then you can tell me... I'd rather look at you in any case!"

Anna gulped as the cab pulled up. This was pure snake oil and she had a juicy apple in her pocket. He looked at her with questioning eyes that ran between her and the opened door. She followed, feeling as if she had gone into free fall from a plane rather than stepping out of a taxi into the busy swirl of Park Lane. As he paid the cab driver, she composed herself. Okay, she was the daughter of Mike Leyton - owner of Leyton Marine - the makers of prestige motor yachts. Clients were always rich and often famous. The flagship Nereus 74 was renowned as fast, luxurious, beautifully sleek and exclusive. When she had last seen her father, the waiting list was at least 2 years. It was this glamorous world of racing car drivers, pop stars, sports icons, celebrity and privilege, on which she had turned her back - choosing instead the hard streets of Brixton and her own quest for respect and success.

The doorman stood aside and nodded respectfully. She caught a look of recognition in his eye as he watched them. Evidently he knew this guy. They walked to the bar. He was several inches taller than her and broad as a barn door. As she kept up with him she sensed his animal power but also his gracefulness. This was no business man - or if he was - he was completely wasted. Around him was an air of subtle expensive cologne - but beneath that a hint of male - a slight chemical whisper that had carried on the winds and tides across time and evolution. This was a lone bull with no ring in his nose.

She ordered vodka - not something she would normally drink - but so what? None of this was real! She had stepped out of her life and soon she would have to retreat like the tide. He sipped a small beer. The glass looked ridiculous in his large hand. He smiled and gave her a look that she caught and followed like a slow waltz. As he held her eyes she swallowed - realizing that warm and deep within, she couldn't stop her physical and emotional response. She sat cross-legged, shifting slightly in her seat, pressing her legs together more firmly knowing that her awareness and focus was sharpening and despite herself she was experiencing a delicious teasing pleasure - God she was simply letting herself go! She had boarded the roller coaster and it was clicking up the slope towards some kind of ride.

"I'm Frederic - Freddie La Salle," he told her, offering his hand to shake. She took it and felt her hand disappear into his warm palm.

"I'm Anna Leyton."

He continued to hold her hand. She felt the strength and gentleness of his grip and did nothing to resist - could do nothing - wanted to do nothing.

"Could it be that you come from the family of Leyton Marine?"

"Well yes - you could say I'm the boss's daughter."

"So if I want a Nereus 74 I can go straight to the front of the line!" he joked - or maybe not joked. As he spoke she realized that his French accent had slipped again from Paris chic to a relaxed Californian. She'd already figured that one. She played along.

"I thought you were French!"

"My mother is American - I live in France and work often in the USA."

"So all that 'lost little French boy' was a scam."

"Of course," he replied in a mocking French accent, "you cannot blame a man when suddenly from out of a clear blue sky in the pouring rain he meets such a woman who tries to muscle him out of his taxi..."

Anna laughed at the pantomime accent and coy expression that looked so out of place on his strong face and scarred brow that had to have a violent origin.

"What's your line of work anyway Frederic - comedian - shepherd - conman?"

"Few people are what they seem - life is an acting job. Truth is a line like the Equator. To the South lies the tropic of exaggeration, to the North is the tropic of forgetfulness," he teased with those smiling dark brown eyes.

Now - what the hell was this stuff? Philosophy - obviously well rehearsed. How could he know anything of her? Clearly he was aware of Leyton Marine and also of the waiting list for a Nereus 74. Did he know her father, or any details of her family?

"So you tested a Nereus 74?"

"Well, I went on board - she was beautiful - there was no time for a sea trial."

"And are you still in the market?"

"Certainly - I have an important deal next month - but after that - it will be play time."

"Who showed you round the boat in Cannes?" she asked, desperate to know what he might recall. With this type of serious client, almost certainly her father would have been involved.

"I think I met someone called Mike... yes it was Mike."

Her thoughts raced through all the possibilities - he had probably spoken to her father and even if he had made small talk about his family, odds were that this confident self-aware stranger wouldn't have taken it all in. Anyway, he wouldn't have told a potential client that his daughter was a cop given that a good number of clients had no love of the law.

"If he could have sold me the boat I'd have bought it that day."

"I'll call my father."

"And you will supervise my sea trial personally?"

Hang on Mister Smoothie... she couldn't go down this route.

"There are good sales people at all our offices - I don't have a demonstration boat in London."

"Perhaps I should call Mike - um - your father...?"

Adrenalin was squeezing into her blood.

"I'll fix it," she said, slowly downing the last of her vodka and hoping she appeared calm.

Okay - she had lied about her job - she could cover it if her father would go along with the deception. None of this mattered. She was never going to see him again. Her father could call him and explain that she had had to sell a boat to the king of some place. Some place with a king!

"If you sell me a Nereus 74 you will be Daddy's Best Girl," he teased, adding a theatrical wink.

"I am already," she fired back sharply, suddenly realizing that losing the chance to sell a cool £2.5 million cruiser would definitely not please Daddy. This guy was too pushy - as if she could be influenced by money!

"Give me your business card Miss Leyton - I'll call you to fix all the details."

Business cards - sure - every sales person always has a pocket full! She thought swiftly on her feet. She could hardly give him a police one.

"I was at a meeting this afternoon and handed them all out so I have none left just now... I was not expecting..."

"A rude stranger who hijacked your taxi!" he interjected.

"Not so rude," she replied with a look at his masculine face, his tough looking jaw, his bull-like neck and those gentle brown eyes. Although his manner exuded confidence almost to a point of arrogance, those eyes shone out a deep kindness. Everything warned her off this guy. Everything she felt as a woman was sweeping her onwards - as if she had fallen into a raging river of warm seductive water where it was useless to struggle. He finished his beer. She declined his offer of second vodka... but boy did she need one.

"So, I'll let you go and take your number?" he suggested.

She scribbled her personal cell phone number on a coaster. He took it and stood up, towering above her. His shoulders were twice the width of hers. She found herself staring at his lower abdomen and waist. He had no stomach but was ridged and flat. A little lower was the bulge of his bull credentials. She forced herself to look up and then stood. As if it were the most natural thing in the world he moved beside her and placed his hand on her back.

"We must find you a taxi."

She felt the sheer size and strength of him. Her composure wobbled on a knife-edge. However she dressed it up, she wanted him, not that he was gonna get that information. He had made no hard play for her. The most dangerous thing in a crook is patience - she knew that. It was screaming at her.

The doorman stepped out to hail a cab. Anna looked up and allowed herself to hold his eyes for a little longer than was quite polite and edged towards brazen, She felt a sweet tickle of excitement. A taxi pulled in.

"Well - thanks for the drink - and the entertainment."

Without speaking he moved to face her and then lowered his chin to kiss one cheek and then the other. The brush of his lips jolted her, sending a current sparking and screaming down through her body, lighting up everything it touched.

"Forgive me..." he began, obviously aware of her response, "these things are normal in France."

Bloody hell - did he think she didn't know that? She watched his lips as he spoke, longing that he would bring them back to her cheeks, to her lips, to anywhere! God it had been so long...

"I'll call tomorrow - it has been lovely to meet you Anna."

"I'll look forward to it Freddie," she replied, hearing her own voice as if it belonged to someone else.

He turned back into the hotel and was gone. She leaned back in the taxi and let out a deep lungful of air. Dear Lord - had she gone nuts? How it had felt though - to be aware of a forgotten joy inside her. For a few moments she had pushed away from that blank plain where dark beasts could roar out of the long grass at any second. For an instant once again she was at the wheel of that car, controlling the drift into the corner. Ahead of her the bandit car spun out as a terrified kid lost control...

Freddie La Salle watched the cab pull away from behind the hotel window. He didn't want her to see his interest. He checked the number she had given him and moved to the lobby payphone and dialed. As she answered he hung up. It was her - the correct number. He smiled and gave a little nod of satisfaction. Never had he seen such a girl. The beauty of her was a delicious ache. In her presence he had felt a surge of desire and a sense of protectiveness he couldn't define. Something was there in her that he recognized. Some hint of his own regret. OK - he needed a girl on his arm, a girl was always part of the plan. Now she was gone there was so much more he could have said - maybe shared - maybe explained.

One day there would be a girl who could share the truth of things. Lucky she wasn't a cop. If there were cops like that he'd have joined the force years ago. When he had seen her in the street he had had to act before she was swirled away into the gray London night.

How a split second in life could change everything. How well he knew the joy and sorrow that could flow from a chance moment. He took out his cell phone and called his driver. The poor guy was probably still waiting for him outside Scotland Yard.

Chapter 2

The phone jolted her from the nightmare. She thought for a moment to ignore it. Few people had her personal number - other than her family and of course her ex-lover Commander Beaumont Locke of Scotland Yard. As the caller clicked off, she pushed the mobile back in her pocket and rested her head on the seat. Probably a random wrong number. If she had time tomorrow she would check it out.

On and on the lives of unknown strangers rolled and swarmed along the Edgeware Road and Kilburn High Road. She was tired but had never felt more alive! By chance she had met this ridiculous chancer and experienced a brief out-of-body experience. Just in an instant her perception of life had changed. She'd always been inclined to rash decisions. How well she knew the price. Now things were real and she had to organize her actual life and career and maybe deal with the consequences of her deliberate dishonesty.

She paid the driver and took the stairs to her flat. Even though it was going to cost her twenty years salary and took half her pay each month, it was only a tiny flat – four small rooms above a tanning salon. She had refused all help from her family. What she had was her own. It wasn't much.

She slipped out of her coat, poured a good glass of Pinot Grigio and headed for the bedroom. She wanted to think and to strip off the grime and gray of the London day. She would shower and then get an early night.

She let her charcoal business suit and cream silk blouse fall carelessly to the ground. She sat down on the bed wearing nothing but her ivory satin underwear. She released her bra and let her full firm breasts fall free like a sigh. For a moment she lay back and swung her legs onto the bed, staring at the ceiling. She ran her hands comfortingly across her belly.

For all the urgent complication of the jingle-jangle day, she was flesh and a beating heart. For the first time in nearly a year she felt herself alive and warm, aware of the pulse and thrill of the life that was in her body. She thought of the enigmatic Freddie, some kind of con man she knew but still with his laughing eyes and strength. No man had ever touched her soul in the way that he had. Everything about him was like a rhythmic stroke - his cheesy humor, his powerful hands - creating a soft force that pushed everything aside and caressed her feminine core. The wine and the vodka shook hands in her empty stomach. Ok - she was drinking too much.

How she hated this loneliness knowing that at any moment her mind could flip back in time. She had no lover although often enough men had told her of her beauty or at least wanted to get in her knickers. No one had ever got this close, not reached the power of her responses that she knew she possessed, yet withheld. This man had no concept of knocking on doors. He had a key and would walk right into her, would know her rhythms, would dance and burrow within her, pulse and share ecstasy with her. This she knew now as if she were the first ever woman to know true oneness with a man. Her loneliness oppressed her and for a few moments she could lose herself. She felt the jolt of her own touch as she focused on her pleasure. This had always been her small secret delight until the crash had wiped out her desire. Now she was flying in circles up and up and up and losing control. It had been so long... just so bloody long.

The pleasure sank away into nothing, like a beautiful wave crashed onto sand, disappearing without a trace. She felt the chill of the air and found herself in tears. Sounds rose from the street and shadows of street lamps patterned her solitary room. She let the tears come silently and turned her face into her pillow. She had always held herself above fully giving in to a man, and now she had let the image of a stranger overwhelm her. No one would ever know. He would never know. She tried to analyze her feelings. Sure she had felt a strong sexual response - but she had felt a longing not only for sex, but for love mixed with her own need to give love. She dreamed briefly of his face - how she had wanted to touch him tenderly and know his soul and being. The absence of him left her reaching out and finding nothing. Now she felt empty. This was not her - not the

Detective Inspector Anna Leyton of Interpol.

She got up and switched on the TV. She needed the sound of its company, but rarely watched. She pulled the curtains, showered and fixed a sandwich. A sense of barrenness drifted like an encircling mist around and within her. She wrapped herself in her dressing gown and put on her slippers. She brushed her long raven hair and cleaned the make up from her creamy skin and deep gray blue eyes.

She had cried - for the first time in months she had allowed feelings to surface. It had been almost a year since her split with Beaumont Locke. At last she felt as if she had moved on and that she could begin to put away at least one episode of her life. Her mind flashed back five years. There had been a murder - and if ever a murder could ever be routine, this was as close as it got. A story of drugs and gangs on the streets of South London had left a youth stabbed and dead on the pavement. She had been a young Detective Sergeant for whom this had been just another file. No one doubted who had done it, but as always a wall of silence and fear sheltered the killers.

Just at this time, questions of gang crime had been raised in Parliament. Police bosses scrambled to get their names on TV and their own heads off the block. Commander Locke of the Scotland Yard murder squad travelled down to South London with his entourage and personal driver. Anna first saw him on the steps of Brixton Police Station with his handsome face to camera. His hair was graying at the temples but otherwise dark and wavy, touching his collar. He wore his uniform for the media but removed his peaked cap so that the public could see his strong suave features, his smile, and accept his unctuous assurances that Law and Order would always prevail. It looked like he believed it - but he'd not spent much time behind a riot shield. Once you've seen a mob running wild, human life is a different concept. Once you've nicked an old dear dragging a fridge out a broken shop window you really understand the psychology of the impulse buy.

As the cameramen and journalists fled with their scoops "Brixton Cops Baffled - Yard Called in" Beaumont Locke made for his temporary office and changed into his double-breasted pin-stripe suit, white shirt with blue collar and matching blue handkerchief flopping from his top pocket. A few minutes later, Anna was seated in his office. She smiled at his name - Beau Locke…he looked too serious to follow her drift.

"You don't want me here, I don't want to be here - let's solve this and go home," he boomed in an upper class English tone, "full report Sergeant - Shoot!!"

Anna bridled at this arrogant monster, yet at the same time was drawn to his sheer self assurance. She gave her report while he leaned back in his chair, appraising her, taking in her willowy beauty and mysterious gray blue eyes. When she had finished he looked at her directly.

"Good girl," he exclaimed with an irritating and patronizing clap, "You're going a long way in your career my dear... or should I say 'Cher', looking at your beautiful hair - dinner together at 8."

"Well..." she began.

"Well Sir!" he corrected.

"Well Sir - 8 will be fine," she said, swallowing her anger.

Within a month they were lovers. Commander Locke - a man destined for the top. 35 years old, Oxford graduate in law and politics, was already divorced from his high flying lawyer wife.

The affair had been just that - an affair - wedged between their careers and egos. For her it had been a release from a detective's life - the tyranny of piss stench stairwells, the halitosis of lies. She knew that she had never been an equal partner - had always been at his command. He had never asked to be called Sir in bed - but if he had, it would not have surprised her.

Then came that day. That day. That second. That lifetime of "if onlys" that would play and play again in her head. How she had been proud of her promotion to Inspector, even though it meant a return to uniform service for a year. She had had no need to chase those kids…no need to push them to... to their death. There she had said it again. Beaten herself with it again. And what a failure he had been! How she had needed him and how he had rowed away from her sinking ship when it looked like his career could be tainted by her troubles. She had stood alone when the mob had brayed for her head. He had scrambled away down the back stairs.

Her mind turned back to Freddie - the silly jokes, his philosophical remarks about truth, the arousing lick of his glance, his wounded brow and gentle brown eyes. That place in her soul that she had sought herself and wondered if it even existed - he had known and caressed in an instant. Something had been released within her and she would never be the same. And hell - she had lied, maybe damaged her father's business and could even have compromised her career - and all because for a few moments she had wanted to be just Anna.

Chapter 3

She slept fitfully, disturbed by fragmenting images of Freddie La Salle and her father. She imagined them together discussing the Nereus 74 motor cruiser over a glass of wine. He was telling the younger man about his detective daughter who had turned her back on the family business, preferring to fight criminals on the streets of London. How she had sat alone in the cells awaiting the verdict at the end of her trial for manslaughter...

She awoke with a start. It was 4 am and outside the traffic still bundled and buzzed through the night and into the dawn. The harsh light from the street lamps patterned her room. The wail of sirens brought her mind back to her real current life. How often she had floored the throttle of a patrol car hurtling through the streets of London... just that once too often. She saw the flames, heard the screaming voices. Maybe she should talk to someone... maybe she should get on with her job... maybe this guy...

In a few hours she would be at a briefing for her new assignment. An international squad had formed to combat the many headed monster of organized crime. In its latest incarnation, the internet allowed billions of dollars to be laundered through anonymous gambling. The money hatched in the swamps of drugs, prostitution, people trafficking and illegal weapon sales was set to work in pursuit of even bigger gains. Sports events could be fixed, players bribed or intimidated, officials corrupted. Huge amounts of cash flowed around the worlds of sport. Players could become the property of criminals. Just in the last few weeks football, cricket and tennis had been hit with revelations and scandals. The London Olympics were scheduled for 2012. The British and International governments wanted not only a level playing field, but also a clean one. She would know more after the briefing, but broadly their task would be to identify the criminals and infiltrate the networks inside sport.

As she took the tube to Vauxhall she was both excited and apprehensive. She was about to meet the other members of the team who would be from all over the world. She had dressed in a neat dark blue suit with a white blouse. In the end she had chosen high heels, to show off her legs and somehow to reflect her new awareness of herself. For the same reason she had selected her sexiest underwear and had paid detailed attention to her makeup. She told herself it was all because she was meeting the new team. Deep down she knew that it was for someone else - someone she would never see again.

It was a short walk to the National Criminal Intelligence Service offices just off the Embankment in Spring Gardens, near to Lambeth Bridge. The first leaves of autumn drifted along the footway. The pushing tongue of the Thames licked around the pillars of the bridges. Instead of focusing on the meeting, her mind turned to Freddie. Of course he would never phone her. She was just a woman he had met by chance in the street. His looks, easy confidence and obvious wealth would mean that there would always be admiring females on hand. How could she let herself dream that there had been a special spark between them? For one stolen hour she had come to life and now it was time to get back to business. She smiled at the way he had put on the heavy accent, took a deep breath and bit her lip as she recalled the maleness of his presence when he had kissed her cheek. She looked out at the sunlight catching the muscle of the river currents, thinking of his large powerful hands and the depth that hinted behind his brown eyes. Everything around had reminders of him. For a minute she stopped and took in the view. She let the picture of him fill her, feeling her body begin to respond. This was crazy! She had met this guy for about an hour and for sure he had some kind of dangerous agenda. He had swept her defenses aside and had simply invaded. The thought of him was like an urgent profound stroking within her body that wouldn't stop.

She was first to arrive at the office, grabbed a coffee from the machine and took it directly to the conference room. She rarely bothered with breakfast beyond an espresso doppio. Next to arrive was a pretty bottle blonde woman of about her own age. For a couple of seconds they looked at each other in disbelief before letting out a shared squeal.

"Judy... Judy... I don't believe it, I thought your were on maternity leave for another couple of months?"

They hugged and stood back. Anna's thoughts raced back to Brixton Police Station where she and Judy had been the first all girl crew on the emergency response area car Lima 3.

Judy had... well... gone blonde and expanded a little since those days! Anyone taking her for a plump Earth Mother would be making a big mistake. She could drive like a demon and toss a violent man over her shoulder.

"Anna - Ma'am... err," Judy stuttered.

How she hated to be called 'Ma'am'! She had not designed the police rank structure and she had no time for self importance.

"Anna... plain old Anna or mate for God's sake," she beamed, "it will be great to be on the same team again - but I had no idea."

She continued delightedly. Quickly she got an update on the baby, the three year old and her husband Brian who was a community cop.

"I spotted the assignment at the last minute and managed to rearrange childcare, so we could work together on this new squad. I only heard a couple of days ago that I'd got the job and thought I'd surprise you!"

Other members of the team drifted in. Some were shiny new detectives just out of the box. A couple were world weary old cops, glad to get out of the trenches for a while. The FBI had provided a bank of bright young analysts and a posse of special agents. Around the conference room conversations sprang up in French Italian and American. Anna joined in, well - she knew she was showing off, warming to her role as an Interpol liaison point between all the various groups. Finally the room fell silent. She looked up to see a familiar figure taking his place at the head of the table. Her heart sank and she found herself choking back rage. This had not been billed as part of the show! Her new boss was none other than her rejected ex lover, Commander Beaumont Locke.

He stood by his chair, motioning with his hand in an upward

gesture indicating that everyone should stand in recognition of his rank and importance. Anna glanced across at Judy who returned a scornful roll of her eyes. This man was so in love with his image that if he had been gay, he would have married himself!

Anna suppressed a wave of loathing and cursed herself. She had let him inside her. Together they had dog rolled in the shit of the Love word. Her mind dragged back to that day. That day when she had left the court, cleared of manslaughter. That day when the suddenly present mothers of the dead kids screamed for her blood as the TV cameras focused in on her tears. That day when Commander Locke had tried to crawl back into the henhouse now that the fox was gone.

When everyone had stood up and fallen silent he graciously motioned them all to sit down. In the context of international squads, few senior officers stood on their dignity. Beaumont Locke was a "Sir". It was only a matter of time before the Queen realized he was right and made it official.

Various officers who had already worked on the enquiry for months gave their briefings. Despite her concentration she found herself drifting into a daydream. Freddie was looking into her eyes. His gaze moved to her mouth as he pushed his own lips forward and looked back to her eyes. She raised her chin to receive the warmth and caressing touch of his kiss...

A distant voice was pulling her back into the present. A Chief Inspector from the National Criminal Intelligence Service had been tasked with assigning roles within the squad.

"Detective Inspector Leyton will be responsible for all European police liaison. I have a note that she will report directly to Commander Locke with her own daily briefing," he said in a flat monotone.

Reporting directly to her ex-lover! The rat who had abandoned her then returned wanting sex the day she was safe. So he had fixed the whole deal. He had wanted her dangling on his string. She fired a glance in his direction and saw a smirk living its stinking life on his hateful face. Something venomous twisted in her gut. The fact that she had language skills and the track record as a top detective meant nothing to him. He had engineered her presence there for his amusement and in order to control her. She stared back at him with a contemptuous raise of her eyebrow. He avoided her eyes and looked away. It was a small victory - but a victory.

At last the meeting broke up for lunch. She collected Judy, grabbed a sandwich from the canteen and headed out of the building. The day was bright and clear and they found a bench overlooking the Thames.

"Come on Anna - what's on your mind?" asked Judy.

"Its just, you know after what happened... and having to work for Beaumont again?"

"Well, we all knew Anna," said Judy, touching her arm, "look, it could have been anyone. We're cops honey... we run on reflexes. We can all say if only this or if only that..."

"Maybe I should have gone to jail. Maybe I deserved that."

"That's rubbish Anna... look honey - it's over. It happened."

She smiled tearfully back at her friend. Judy just did not do sentiment.

"Beaumont is a piece of slime... he's got me here out of spite... because I rejected him."

"Well - you can deal with that I'm sure. Are you certain there's nothing else bothering you?" asked Judy with an open sympathetic smile.

Anna took a deep breath, she still felt the same trust and ease in her friend's company. As she thought carefully she checked her mobile in case she had missed any calls. She noticed the mystery number from the previous night.

"Could you get a number checked discreetly?" she asked, scribbling on a business card and passing it to her.

"Of course, but come on Anna. Let's pretend we're on night shift at Brixton and we're sitting up waiting for the next nightmare."

Her mind turned back to how they had shared every danger and every personal secret. Okay - she would not short change her old comrade and anyhow, she needed to talk like never before.

"I met a guy - I met a guy who's left me wondering about everything - about what I am and what I want," she said, relieved to have opened her heart. Just the act of talking about him brought him alive.

"How long have you known him?"

"About an hour."

"About an hour - are you serious? This is strong medicine! Give me the whole gorgeous picture."

Anna gave her the story of their meeting, his humor, his looks and sexual presence. Listening to herself she realized that if there had been no more than this, she would have merely shrugged it off.

"But there was more than that," she continued, "I wanted him completely. I wanted to care and give him everything - really absolutely anything - and I'd only just met him. I felt kind of enslaved and filled with power all at once. But I do know he's some sort of crook."

"God - what's his name? Does he have a brother or at least a close relative?" asked Judy with a theatrical wistfulness.

"Frederic - Freddie, Freddie Freddie, Freddie," she replied letting the name bubble out joyfully as if to say his name brought him alive at her side.

"Freddie... I think I heard that name recently... something Brian said perhaps, but all he does is read the back page of the paper. But heck... what are you going to do?"

"There's nothing to do. I won't hear from him again."

"Do you want to bet on that? We are on the gambling squad," laughed Judy

Anna laughed too, unable to resist the delicious possibility that she would see him again. Judy reached out and gave her hand a reassuring squeeze.

"Look, this guy's gonna call. Just look at you - slim - Miss World looks, educated and from a rich family. Damn near makes me sick!"

"Would you swap lives with me Judy?" she asked seriously.

Her friend looked out across the river and appeared to be thinking before she replied.

"To be honest - no. The two horrors at home drive me nuts and it's an uphill slog to work and be everywhere else. But now it makes sense - at last something makes sense."

"How come?" asked Anna, surprised to have received such a philosophical answer.

"Do you remember all the dead junkies, all those cops and robbers chases, all those desperate folk who'd just been robbed raped or worse? Well, when you hold your baby - all new and innocent with a life ahead where anything is possible - it kinda tells you why we do it - why we care. Anyway that's what they told me on the Home Office woman awareness course. It also tells you that something weighing ten pounds can contain twelve pounds of shit."

Just when you thought Judy had found God she hit you with some excrement. She smiled at her friend. Those dead kids in that car had been babies once. Her own professional life was back on track. Not so long ago she could have been in that big truck on the way to Holloway prison.

They wandered back to the office in the warm sunshine still living on its memories of summer. Their friendship had been re-born and this unexpected reunion meant more to her than she could ever have imagined. Just as they reached the door she felt the vibrating alert of her cell phone. She snatched it out of her pocket and looked at the number. It was an unknown contact with an international prefix of 33. The caller was on a French phone. Her heart leapt and thumped. She stared at the phone without moving. It continued to buzz in her hand. All her conflicting feelings were beginning to shout at once.

"Answer it!" ordered Judy with a bemused frown, "you know you're gonna die if you don't see him again. If he's a crook you can still shag him and then lock him up. It'll only cost you money if he rings off and you have to call him back!"

With that her friend went on into the building and Anna did what she had to do... she pressed the answer button.

"Madame Leyton. I am calling about the boat you have advertised for sale. Is it still available and could I come round to see if it floats?" came a delicious deep voice in a deliberately hammy accent.

Anna laughed with nervousness and at his offbeat humor

"Yes, of course," she stumbled.

"Ok, I will come straight round. I have to leave London tomorrow and maybe I can be sailing back to France if the boat is good?"

"No... look Freddie you can't do that," she replied with a grin in her voice.

"Ooh là là. So you remember me. You must be a top girl - but isn't it usually the sales people who chase the client?"

Her mind raced with all the consequences of her next move. She knew that her plain lust for him would pull her along as if she had no more will than a bottle bobbing in the Thames. Perhaps he had realized that there was something very odd about a sales type with no business cards and who didn't try to close a sale. And come on woman - he just has to be a crook.

"The Nereus sells itself to the right quality of buyer."

"So I must prove my quality eh? Well, we had better fix a date then."

"I'm waiting for a call from my father. He's down in Antibes right now," she lied.

"Well, call him again and you can tell me the result tonight."

The sexy sound of his voice was pressing on all her doors. Maybe she could peep out.

"Tonight?"

"Yes… it is that wonderful period in our lives that will happen between now and tomorrow." he said with such obviousness it was like a wet lick from a Labrador.

And still she was being swept along. She was falling for it for Christ's sake. If she was going to see him - and she knew that she was - she would need to get home, get herself made over, and find some kind of composure.

"It's a kind offer... I have to work quite late - maybe I'll be free at about 8.30."

"I'll pick you up... just give me the address."

She faltered. She didn't want this guy to know her address. She had known him for an hour and she knew nothing about him. She thought quickly. If she knew a date of birth she could check him out with French police. She hated the way her mind had come to work - with everyone under suspicion. If ever he wanted to know why she didn't tell him she was a cop, this would be reason enough.

"I'll be at Queen's Park tube station," she blurted out, knowing that she could walk there easily from her flat.

"Ok - it must be tough selling boats. Be hungry - I have something to show you."

She imagined him holding the phone. His voice soothed and seduced her. She imagined the hard strong feel of his body, the brush of his lips. She brought her mind back to a police check.

"Freddie - what star sign are you?" she asked, hoping she sounded girly.

"What - do you do all this destiny stuff? If you must know - I'm a Gemini - 23rd May. Do I fit with your chart?"

She felt a little ashamed and kind of dirty. He had answered so innocently and openly. Here she was - using an old police trick to get a handle on his ID. When she had met him she had snatched the chance to be simply herself as a woman. She would have to tell him the truth before things went too far.

"Yeah - you fit my chart. Will you be standing at the station?"

"You won't be able to miss me. À bientôt Chérie," he said, and was gone.

God! She was already late. She had to check him out. He was rich - seemingly minted up to his eyes. Certainly he didn't run a corner store or fix washing machines. Any woman would wonder, let alone a Scotland Yard Detective. When a woman wonders it's curiosity, but when an Interpol detective wondered - it was suspicion. She knew that it was against police regulations to mix with anyone undesirable. She smiled at the word since Freddie was the most desirable man she had ever met. One thing she knew - this was no regular guy. And if he were a crook - what would she do or care?

Chapter 4

It was mid afternoon when she got the chance to call Interpol headquarters in Lyon, France. Just as she was about to lift the handset, Judy walked into the office.

"You know that number you gave me to check... the call you received in the taxi last night... it was a payphone in the lobby of the Hilton, Park Lane."

Anna leaned back in her chair. It must have been Freddie, checking out her number to see if she had been straight with him. He was no fool. He was patient and calculating. Would he expect her to lie? The question evoked her big lie that sat like a stone in her heart. When she saw him again she would tell him. She dialed the Interpol number and waited.

"Inspecteur Du Maurier - bonjour."

"Raymond - bonjour," she began, speaking automatically in flawless French, "un petit service s'il vous plaît. Can you run a check on a French National called Freddie La Salle born 23rd May... he's about 34," the line went silent.

"Raymond...?"

"You are serious? You do not need me Anna. Try Google or the Newspapers," chuckled Du Maurier, "I guess you are too busy to read the sports pages?"

"Raymond. Tell me! Who is he?"

"Freddie La Salle, World Cruiserweight Champion - signed yesterday for the final defense of his title."

"A boxer!"

"And some... de plus! Une légende. He's still a pretty boy - but he was badly cut by a head butt in his last fight. I'm guessing you don't follow the fight game Anna?"

"No - never, it's not too kosher - I have to think of my personality profile with the human resources department. I could be denounced," she half joked, knowing that an interest in boxing could mark her as politically incorrect.

"Freddie would tell you it's an art form. He's a bit of a puzzle. He reads philosophy and has written a book about the artist Gustave Courbet. He's a noted art collector. His mother is a Yank and doubles as his manager. His father is the French poet Mathieu La Salle. Freddie has business interests all over the world."

"He doesn't look beaten up... but you're right, there is a mean scar over his right brow," she answered numbly, trying to take in all the information.

"The champion is the guy who hurts the other guy. That cut was his only injury in the ring. A lot of questions were asked."

"Questions?" Anna echoed.

"Certainement... questions of murder and money. I'll e mail you the whole file and note your interest. That way any input or news will get flashed straight to you."

She thanked her colleague and rang off, immediately typing La Salle into the Google window. Dozens of files popped up. She clicked on a fan site. There he was, gloved with hands raised looking out from the ring, blood pouring from a terrible gash over his eye. A headline ran "Le French Professor gets a lesson in pain". Anna winced at the corny pun. She flicked through other web sites, making notes. Freddie La Salle - known as "le Professeur" on account of his careful boxing technique and intellectual tastes. His trip to London was widely examined under the title "A Fight Too Far". He had signed to fight Billy 'The Boulder' Brennan, an up and coming hard man out of New York City. She read on in horror that Freddie was rumored not to have trained for the fight and just wanted a final pay day. The article described Brennan as 'the most dangerous street fighting brawler that he would ever face.'

She hated the thought of him cut and even maimed in a terrible contest. Beneath his humorous and thoughtful manner there must be a brute. She flicked on through pages of him in his champion's belts, flexing his biceps, triceps, quadriceps and pecs. Sure it was tacky, but God! He was gorgeous. There was Freddie with blondes in bikinis, Freddie with babes in grass skirts, Freddie with French film stars - none of whom she knew. How could she never have heard of him? She hadn't seen a movie for years, never read the sports pages and always put her work in front of everything else in her life. Whatever happened - she had to get out more!

The office door opened and she pulled her eyes away from the screen.

"The Commander wants to see you," Judy informed her, adding a flat derision to the word Commander, "he's just so up himself."

"Tell me about it," Anna agreed, her heart sinking at the thought of him. Judy came round and looked over her shoulder at the screen.

"Wah!!!" she exclaimed, "is that him? Are you gonna sort him out - WOW - I would! Is he a sex God or what?"

"That's Freddie, but please keep it to yourself - I just didn't know."

"I knew I'd seen the name. It was on the back of Brian's paper - the one he holds up to his face so I can't talk to him."

Anna saw an icon flash blink the computer monitor. The file from Inspecteur Du Maurier had come in from Interpol France. She clicked the download.

"There's a file on Freddie. Can you open and print for me while I go and see Mister Big?"

"That's not what I heard," laughed Judy suggestively.

Anna smiled, raising her pinkie with a mocking wiggle.

"Don't forget to salute," called Judy as she stepped out.

"Ah - Inspector Leyton," began Beaumont Locke in his most pompous voice, sweeping his hand languidly back through his graying hair and pushing back his leather executive chair. "We need to touch base and set a few targets and parameters. I believe in a consensual approach to individual empowerment. I want to see a developed profile of key performance indicators so that we can roll out a joint action plan."

Without permission Anna sat down and stifled a laugh.

"Obviously you've been on another senior command and control management jargon course," she sneered with an unwavering stare.

He moved his chair forward, "Anna - Darling... it doesn't have to be like this," he sighed gazing up at the ceiling with a patronizing weariness.

"What!" she exploded, "we are over Beaumont. Somehow you have abused your power to get me on this squad. I'll let that ride... just so long as you let me get on with my job and don't use the situation to exercise personal control over me. The squad wanted a European language speaking detective. Well, you got yourself one and that's all you've got Commander Locke. You didn't want to be near me when you thought some shit could stick to you."

He moved back and nodded with narrowed eyes. She knew that he would not risk any politics with her. He was on the way up and needed to stay clean. She had no malice or resentment towards him now. He had shown himself and he knew she knew what he was.

"Let's stick to business Inspector. Everything comes through me first OK," he said stiffly.

"You're the boss - I guess you wouldn't want anyone else to get any glory."

"Don't be impertinent!" he boomed, "no swanning about with half baked continentals. No unofficial liaisons with foreign agencies. I know you have all kinds of pavement café tendencies. This is a Scotland Yard job - and you are a Metropolitan police officer merely on attachment to Interpol - whatever all these internationals want to think."

"Why don't you just stand over me?" she snapped.

"Sir!" he ordered.

"Sir!" she echoed as she stormed from the room.

She could not believe his arrogance. How could she ever have thought that there was something enduring between them? It had been a mistake, but mistakes were sails not anchors. A wind had got up and she was sailing on.

It was six o' clock and she had to get going. Reaching her office she found Judy still there, intently reading the file from Interpol France.

"You gotta read this," she bubbled excitedly, "your man could unlock the whole enquiry."

Anna thought quickly, pushing aside her anger at her ex lover's presence in her life.

"Can you give me the story as we head for the tube?" she breezed, realizing that Judy had two kids at home and was working late out of friendship. All she had on her mind was some kind of fantasy evening with a world boxing champion who was into philosophy, collected art and turned her insides to a warm flow of breathing life. And who had lifted the focus of her life from her past to a continuously evolving present.

Judy grabbed the file and kept pace alongside her.

"Well, his last fight in Marseille attracted a massive amount of gambling on Freddie to lose, even though on form he should have walked it. He was completely on top during the fight when suddenly the other guy butted him and ripped his eyebrow open. The referee had to stop the fight because the blood was pouring into Freddie's eyes. The crowd and a big TV audience had all seen the butt and the ref disqualified the guy and awarded the win to Freddie."

"Is that normal?" asked Anna.

"It can be, but the view was that if the head butt had not been so obvious then the ref would have stopped the fight and the other guy would have won."

"So what did Freddie know?"

"Good question. It looked as if he was going for the win... but why target him? We simply don't know what he knew... but it gets far more complicated," Judy continued excitedly, "Three weeks after the fight the ref ends up dead in the Hudson River. It seems like he had a gambling habit himself and had taken a loan from some sharks. According to his widow he was offered a free pass if he fixed the fight."

"So what went wrong?"

"The other boxer was not too subtle and was very inferior to Freddie. The idea was that the ref would allow a lot of fighting on the inside... you know... that type of mauling where they kinda waltz with the other guys head up their nose. The guy was supposed to clash heads during a clinch. By the fourth round the guy is half dead and probably desperate. So - he just stands back and butts Freddie like it was a Friday night outside the pub. The ref had no choice."

"So why kill the ref?"

"Simple... when the boys called for their cash he told them he had taped the conversation and would go to the FBI."

"Any suspects?"

"Sure. It looks like an old fashioned movie style hit. But the cash and the backing come from anywhere between the North Korean government and the Chinese Triads," laughed Judy.

"I get the picture," commented Anna.

She knew that the internet provided a platform for any amount of criminal liaisons and deals. All manner of dirty cash sloshed around the worlds of internet gambling, drugs, girls and weapons.

"So what does the widow know?"

"She took the greyhound out of town - or at least a ticket was purchased in her name. The internet address of the booker was in New Jersey. I've got a feeling that the widow is keeping her head down or hasn't got a head," said Judy with a professional nonchalance.

At Vauxhall tube station they parted and headed off into the undergrowth of their own lives. She sat down gratefully and pondered how something already difficult had become impossible. And yet - she was going to see him. He had called her and she was going to see him! She was going to feel the thrill of his presence and maybe more - maybe anything.

She closed her eyes and ran through the photos of him glistening and pumped up in his shorts and gloves. He was a modern day gladiator with soft brown eyes and apparently a taste for art. She let everything of the day slip away. Nothing was ever more than this - to be naked and tuned to the rhythm of this Earth and to each other. Falseness was stacked upon falseness, the joy of the moment always soured by the past. She felt again the warm tickling surge deep in her belly and knew that she was responding physically even to the thought of him. For tonight the tongue of lava flow would take her and if that was into his arms - or more - then so it would be. The fuse on the regret circuit had burned out with the overload. And it had just been so long... so bloody long.

Chapter 5

Once back to the flat she had to organize her clothes. She had no idea where they were going - so she had no idea how to dress. There could be nothing worse than being overdressed except perhaps being underdressed and disappointing him. Looking at the photos on his fan website, most of the girls around him wore next to nothing. She showered, thankful that her legs had just been waxed. She rejected any kind of trouser suit. He had not seen her legs and she knew that they were long tanned and shapely. Her size 14 was full and womanly and she was at ease with her body. Her skin was creamy and clear, her hair was raven black, shiny and her eyes gray blue and bright.

She thought to phone Judy for a chat about her dress but decided against it. The poor girl would have enough to do. Finally she selected a purple bias cut satin knee length dress. The shoes were a worry. Would they be dancing? She opted for her silver satin sandals with a bow and medium heels. She chose her sexiest underwear and imagined him slipping it off. She ran her hand down her own forearm as if it were his hand. Sure, she had been very attracted to a man before, had imagined love and had synthesized it so as at least to enter that lovers club where they churned out your sing-along song. But she had never loved, had never been prepared to risk and surrender. Now something inside her was pushing up like a bloom in spring because it was its season and it couldn't stop. It was coming and there was no escape from the beauty and suffering of love.

Hurriedly she dashed around the flat making sure that there was nothing to reveal her real life, just in case, just in the impossible case of him coming there. Tonight she would have to tell him everything or there could be no future. Probably there could be no future anyway.

She waited at the Queens Park tube station, looking up and down the street that any criminal would have recognized as the manner of a cop. She stepped back and tried to relax. Late homecoming workers pushed almost blindly out into the street. A group of boys in hoods waited in the entrance smoking and spitting. One of them looked across at her and said something to his mates. There was a chorus of brash laughter and they all turned to face her, looking her up and down. Despite all she knew she felt uneasy and threatened. If this went on for a couple of minutes things could go very wrong indeed. Mentally she rehearsed a focused karate chop with the side of her hand up under the nose of an attacker. This was not what she had wanted. Why had she been so coy and not just given him her address?

A black Cadillac Stretch limo pulled into the curb. She watched the boys plant their eyes on it. Freddie stepped out from the back and held the door open.

"Madame... I am lost in the big city... you can 'elp me perhaps?" he said in his pantomime French accent. She went to the car as he took a step towards the hooded boys. No one met his gaze. He was about 6 feet 3 inches, 200 lbs and had total self assurance. If even she had felt the heat of his presence, these kids were about to get burned. In a second they had glanced at each other and had gone. He stepped back into the car and sat beside her, "Maybe they were rude kids?" he commented, "they have not so many chances in life perhaps."

He looked fantastic in a deep blue casual jacket, open neck striped blue shirt and black pleated trousers that fitted tightly around his honed waist and buttocks. She settled down into the sumptuous red leather of the Cadillac. The in car music system played a gentle piano sonata.

"I'm so happy you could meet me," he said softly, picking up her hand as if he simply could, as if he had that automatic power. She smiled acknowledging her assent. She let the mood of the music relax her as the huge vehicle cruised smoothly across London. He kept her hand, stroking each of her fingers tenderly with his powerful hands as if he was mapping every fold of her. She felt as if she were a precious object that he was gently exploring. She wanted to speak. There was so much that had to be said but the mood and his presence filled her.

"We have forgotten to talk of boats," she said dreamily at last, looking into his eyes which were as warm as his touch. He closed his eyes slowly and she watched the sweep of his long lashes.

"You look - no - you are - so beautiful," he said softly.

She felt a surge of feeling that rippled upwards through her body in waves. She reached out and touched his scarred brow as if to take away the reality of it and of his violent life. And then - then he tilted up his chin and pushed a nuzzling kiss into the palm of her hand. Something beyond desire or anything she recognized as human both filled and drained her, leaving her motionless.

"Merci," he whispered.

"Pourquoi?

"Pour ta tendresse."

She was about to ask him what he meant but being with him had no meanings. Meanings were what had happened in her life before Freddie.

They had stopped in Chelsea, just off Sloane Square. The driver came round and opened the door. They stepped out, hand in hand. Two camera flashes startled her.

"Just a couple of paps - they have their job to do and anyway... I am not supposed to be with anyone else," he commented casually.

Anna dragged her mind back to the present. Paparazzi - she did not want her picture in the papers. She brushed aside her anxiety. Nothing was going to interfere with these few stolen hours.

They were outside a restaurant 'La Galerie' which was clearly exclusive. A waiter opened the door as they entered.

"I hope you like it here. If not there is no one else to blame," he smiled.

"You own it?"

"Well, you know, ma mère - she saw it as an investment."

They took a secluded reserved table. The walls were decorated with fabulous paintings, everything from classical to cubist. He picked up on her interest.

"Only a few are originals - I commission copies of works I admire."

Above them hung a full size copy of a Bronzino that she knew from the National Gallery. Venus was stealing Cupid's arrow because of his wayward aim. Father Time was pulling back the curtain of Truth. She felt like a diver on the high board. She had to jump...

"Freddie - I know who you are now. When we met we did not know anything of each other and..."

"And it was so beautiful. It was the same for me. Now I know you only want to sell me a boat.." he joked.

"No. No," she insisted, "you know it is not like that, it's just that.."

"I'm a brute... you have discovered how I live."

"I never said that - I don't care about that."

"Things have gone that way Anna. Maybe I would change it but I live with it you know. Shall we eat?"

His tone had hardened and she felt that he had withdrawn from her. There was some place in his soul where she could not go and anyway, there was nowhere to go after tonight.

"Are you eating garlic?" he asked with a smile, "in case..."

"Are you expecting a kiss?" she said, feeling her heart leap.

"I do not presume..."

"You may presume Monsieur," she whispered, "and yes - I want garlic and hot spice."

He ordered champagne - Veuve La Salle from his own vineyard. The superb meal - carpaccio of venison with truffle sauce, roasted salmon with rose petal harissa, white chocolate panna cotta with blackberry coulis - blended with his presence. She floated in time, watching his powerful hands, the strength of his neck and shoulders beneath his jacket. His movements were light and graceful but hinting at a restrained physical danger. They left aside talk of boxing or boats. They chatted about art, often in French. More and more they fell in step. As she lifted her knife, so did he. When she looked up at his face, she found his gaze coming up to meet hers. Somehow they were entwining without touch, following a choreography laid down in time for lovers. He was proud of his Michelin star and had a good knowledge of food and fine wine.

"My mother is a brilliant woman - she deals with the business side of things," he told her.

"And your father?" she asked. He hesitated a little.

"Well, it wasn't a perfect match - he is a poor university teacher you know, but he never..."

"Never?" she prompted.

"Never wanted a boxer for a son. He is a serious poet, what you call an intellectual."

"Not even with your fame and success?"

"Especially not those things," he said sadly.

She reached across the table for his hand. He returned her squeeze.

"Too bad," he shrugged, "I cannot say that my mother wanted it - but it has brought so many things - obviously money, respect and freedom."

Once again the weight of her big lie sat like a stone in her heart. He was talking so openly about his life and she could not return the same. She would tell him now!

The message alert of her mobile dragged her attention away. She apologized and pulled it out of her bag. It was a short report from the

London bureau of Interpol. "Note your interest in La Salle. Asian sources report huge money going on Brennan to win. Looks like something is cooking up around this fight. Have a nice week-end."

Inwardly she nailed down her responses. She looked at him, wondering what he knew. Her best way of finding out was to hang in there - but how could she? Why didn't she simply ask him? He was looking at her with a slightly raised questioning eyebrow.

"The boat business - or something romantic?" he probed.

"No, of course nothing like that. It's my father."

"Ah, you have arranged the sea trial."

"Yes," she lied, slipping further down the slope of deceit, but grateful to get off the ropes.

"When could you be available?"

"I am in France all week and then I must fly to California for training."

"Isn't the fight in New York?"

"Yes, but my mother is in Monterey," he said, nodding ruefully.

"So, I will fix a day at the end of the week and call you."

"OK," he beamed, "So we will meet again."

"We have not said Good Night," she replied with a knowing glance.

He grinned. Small wrinkles were beginning to deepen at the corners of his eyes. Looking at him left her melted. She tried to focus on the significance of the message. Freddie was on the radar of her enquiry. Inspecteur Du Maurier had logged her interest in his file and now she was professionally linked to him. If she had to investigate him she could hardly do it as his lover. She couldn't trick her way into his heart or compromise her career by having an affair with a suspect. She ought to tell him and leave - but lose the chance of a major advance in the case. She could work to show his innocence just as well as his guilt.

"We could go dancing?" he suggested tenderly. She looked back into his eyes.

"Can't I keep you just to myself?" she replied, realizing she was being blatant and shameless. Despite herself she was slipping further and further beyond an invisible line. He still didn't know where she lived. She could change her mobile number in the morning. Like a fool she had told him she sold boats and was linked to Leyton Marine. She could never have known that her work would involve him. In the back of her mind she realized that he was in danger both from crooks and in the ring. Now she had lied about the message from her father and was committed to a sea trial on a Nereus 74 in a week's time.

She swallowed the last of her wine and with it everything that swirled around her. She - they - had tonight and if there were never another night in the world, she had until morning to fulfill something she knew was her destiny.

She watched the other diners, wondering how their affairs intertwined. There would be few with such a complex lives. He took her hand across the table. His touch thrilled and electrified her body, merging her emotions with a physical longing.

"I saw you and the world was a different place," he said in a slow deliberate deep tone.

Her eyes were locked with his, both of them searching within the other for understanding.

"You think I am trying it on - I cannot blame you."

She wanted to say that she did not care. She was bursting and fought to control her breathing.

"It does seem pathetic to say that we don't know each other. It seems like we do - but how can we?" she sighed helplessly.

"So our project is to discover each other... it may last a long long time," he replied.

Inwardly she winced. He was right and the poor guy was being deceived.

"I do not want this night ever to end Freddie - can I tell you that and hope you'll understand?" she urged softly, hoping that one day in the future he might untangle her meaning.

"Then we need not end it. We can be our own island... and all those ships can sail by. I won't wave or light a fire if you don't."

It was not fair. He was so beautiful.

"Freddie - I have a small place. We could be - we could be together until the world sweeps us up again," she said, searching his eyes.

"A strange man in your home - you will not be afraid?"

She caught his train of thought. He really was a gentleman. She knew that she was going absolutely for broke, taking all manner of risks. The moment she had touched his brow in the car and had felt his lips kiss the palm of her hand, she knew that her life had changed and would never be the same.

"Something brought us together Freddie."

He nodded agreement and stroked the inside of her wrist.

"And you are going to say that you should not..." he began.

"Should not sleep with a man I've only just met," she added into his silence.

He looked up and let out a sigh.

"I feel we knew each other since always and our bodies might just be catching up," he said with a shrug.

A few minutes later they settled back into the limo. The evening had turned to night yet the city was vibrant with sound and lights.

"London is so beautiful," she said, taking the chance to normalize the situation with a shred of small talk.

Freddie opened the partition and spoke to the driver. The car pushed on to Parliament Square and pulled over on Westminster Bridge.

"We have a moment to look at your beautiful city," he said.

They stepped out. He put an arm around her shoulder as they looked downstream towards the City and Charing Cross. She felt his strength and power. Lights danced in the river. He turned her to face him. She ran her hand down his shoulder and arm feeling the round contour of his hard muscle. He pulled her against his strong body. She felt his hand move to her cheek. She watched his face as his fingers gently traced the shape of her lips. Just as she could bear it no more he raised her chin and kissed her with a melting softness. He held her lower lip in his, gently brushing it with the tip of his tongue. His powerful hand caressed her cheek with an impossible tenderness. This was the kiss - the kiss that made her whole and that she had always known was there but had been missing from the pattern of the universe. She felt exhilarated and calmed by a feeling of harmony.

Beneath his clothing she could feel that she had aroused him and let the core of her own pleasure press against his sculpted muscular thigh. The world slipped away as two lovers kissed on a bridge at the heart of the great city. Still caressing her cheek, his lips traced the line of her delicate nose and kissed the closed lids of her eyes with such gentle passion that she groaned. He caught the sound and with his own shuddering sigh began to nibble her neck and pull her more tightly against him. She felt her legs almost buckle and let herself press helplessly against him, even more aware of his strength. He was a rock, yet a living loving rock that could give and receive love. She pushed the L word away. Love was a weight that this fragile moment could not yet carry.

"That was beyond a kiss," he purred into her ear.

The joy of his lips on her neck still tingled through her as they returned to the car. She leaned her head on his shoulder and then on his chest as he stroked her long black hair. Feelings of warmth flooded through her. She pushed her lips through a gap in his shirt, kissing and licking the smooth muscle of his chest. She ran her hand along the inside of his thigh, pressing towards and teasing his desire. She knew what she wanted to do, longed to do. She knew that she could bring him to physical ecstasy and satisfy her own longing to abandon and let go.

Her body boiled with desire as he lifted her head upwards and kissed her lips, gently reaching across and letting his hand softly brush her breast. Her nipple had already tightened towards his touch as a connection fired downwards into the heat of her longing belly. She was losing control, involuntarily letting her legs slip apart, sensing her lust mixing with his rock hard need for her. She needed his touch deep inside her. A craving gushed from her soul and connected to him through his tender kiss. Their tongues shared an ecstasy of new knowledge, hinting at everything that could flow between them.

She felt the car pull up. They were at her flat. She regained control of herself, yet she brushed his cheek with her hand as if to reassure herself that he was real.

"Coffee?" she enquired knowingly.

"Keeps me awake," he replied in a relaxed drawl with half closed eyes.

"Too bad," she answered, taking his hand.

Freddie opened the hatch and spoke to his driver, telling him to have an early night with his wife and to forget where he had left him. Just for emphasis he added a £50 note and gave the guy a pat on the back.

As the Cadillac powered away, Anna was glad that it was dark and he could not see the urban untidiness of her home. Inside she had created an environment, but outside, the bins and boxes of the city crowded in around her.

The lounge was tastefully understated with prints of Lempicka, Picasso and a Caravaggio. A coffee table guide to the Musée d'Orsay in Paris lay on the beige leather sofa. He pulled her to him and kissed her. The firmness of his body thrilled her as she pressed against him. She pulled back and threw off her jacket. He slipped off the shoulder straps of her dress which slid away silently to the floor.

"Que t'es belle," he groaned, unhooking her bra.

She pulled down on his shoulders, indicating he should sit on the sofa. As he lowered himself she leaned over him so that her breasts brushed his face. He drew a nipple into his mouth while she ran her hands back through his short cropped hair that felt like fur.

His mouth moved to her navel. She sighed with desire for him as her legs seemed to lose all strength. She wanted him now, wanted to feel him move inside her. In one smooth sweep he stood and lifted her off her feet. She felt literally possessed. The hard muscle of his arms against her back and thighs thrilled her. As his lips pressed urgently against hers, he carried her to the bedroom and lay her down on the bed. Light from the street lamps illuminated the room with an orange twilight.

She sat up and unbuttoned his shirt - at last able to touch his naked rippled flesh. Then she released his belt, setting free the surging spring of his manhood. He quickly pulled away his clothing and lay beside her. Only her knickers remained. His lips joined hers in a gentle kiss as his hand began to stroke the moistening silk. A pulse of pure joy filled her body. Now his hand slipped inside the fabric and effortlessly threw aside her last barrier. He began to tease the apex of her inner hood while his lips moved to her breast and drew her in to his mouth. Her nipples swelled and puckered with desire as he pulled an invisible thread through from her longing belly. She felt the rhythmic motion of his hand circling the secret petals of her bud. Her pleasure trapped her in self absorbed rapture. She opened herself to his touch and felt his teasing finger seeking out her source.

"Anna - I have to know you," he whispered as he brought his mouth tenderly to her inner folds. She grasped his head and groaned his name as she felt his soft tongue run across her tight little button, teasing and tempting with gentle circles and deep sucking kisses.

"My sweet juicy baby," he murmured as her tension built up and up. Despite herself she was letting go and coming against his soft lips, letting her soft juicy flesh press into him, losing herself in joy.

"My lover... you are wonderful," he said as he pulled away and moved above her. She could see the width and power of his shoulders and ran her hands over his iron muscles. After shocks still shuddered through her as he filled her. She let out a squeal as his strength took hold of her belly, moving in long slow thrusts. She reached behind to feel his rock hard tireless buttocks. She bucked upwards as orgasm flooded through her again. Her lips found his and he paused to caress her lips and tongue. Then his thrusts pushed into her again as waves of pleasure spilled one upon another.

She felt him begin to tense and push more and more deeply, more urgently. She pulled him into her, arching her back and coming as he let go his seed, mixing and flowing in ecstasy as one being, thrusting and drenching in waves and spasms of love and joy - as if woven together as two streams rushing and gushing into one river.

He moaned deeply as at last he lay back and she snuggled against him, her head on his rippled chest. He kissed the top of her forehead and stroked her hair. His other hand ran behind her neck and cradled her shoulder. His male scent caressed and possessed her. From the street sounds and lights hinted at an outside world. For these precious hours she felt separated and safe. Soon enough all manner of worries would have to be faced.

"I think I got carried away," she sighed dreamily.

"You are beautiful - it's that complicated and that simple," he replied, squeezing her more firmly.

"Consequences..." she began.

"You wanna talk philosophy," he teased.

"No, not now," she whispered.

A mellow drifting silence wrapped them. She ran her hand idly over the honed ridges of his stomach, aware that she was again awakening her desire. But it was a desire mixed with tenderness. She propped herself up on an elbow and touched the scar above his eye, lowering her lips in a searching kiss. He stroked her breast as her nipple hardened and pressed against his chest. Suddenly the fear of him being injured again bubbled out of her.

"Do you have to fight again?"

"Of course."

"Could you not pull out?"

"What the hell for - in case I get cut? I'm a boxer Anna. I fight in public for money. That's what I do and what I have done with my life."

Her thoughts raced. Just what did he know of the gambling or the death of the referee? Soon enough all these different worlds would collide and she could not reveal what she knew.

"A champion retires in the ring, win or lose," he continued.

She sensed his determination and also some kind of wall within him that she could not yet penetrate.

"This Billy Brennan is dangerous isn't he?"

"Not as dangerous as a Leyton powerboat if you do not handle it properly - so you had better instruct me my gorgeous lover," he joked, obviously keen to steer her away from boxing.

She lay back. He seemed to sense that he had raised a barrier to her and stroked her cheek.

"Chérie - there is more to all of this than you know - more than I can tell you."

His deep brown eyes fixed on hers and even in the dim light she could see a slight note of pleading in his expression.

"In this short time you have come into my life and things seem different now. I would like you to know everything - but this last fight must be and after there is the rest of time for us."

She cuddled against him, aware of her pleasure as she felt the hard defined flesh of his velvety thigh. A surge of love for him ran helplessly across her mind like a cloud shadow on a field of corn. She would have to think but now was not the moment.

"You haven't closed the boat deal," he murmured idly.

"Let's not talk about work," she said as she began to kiss her way down the rippled six pack muscles of his stomach.

When she awoke it was dawn merging into day. Thankfully it was Saturday. He still slept as she slid out of bed and tiptoed to the lounge. Quickly she e-mailed her father: "Papa - I have come across potential client for Nereus 74. Can we come to Antibes end of the coming week for a sea trial? Complicated story - will call later. Anna x."

As long as she arranged the boat excursion she should be able to keep all the balls in the air for a little longer. Even so she was dragging her father into her lie and it was by no means certain that he would go along with it.

She heard a sound and felt his lips kiss her hair and swung round to see him behind her wearing only his briefs.

"Complicated indeed," he purred, "had you not told him? - I thought you had fixed it."

Her heart thumped.

"I've been talking to the office - I'm keeping him up to date," she lied, closing her lap top. She knew that if he thought about it he would realize she was lying but he seemed to accept it. Perhaps she should just tell him now that she was an Interpol detective and very possibly she could end up on his case? Perhaps not!

She fixed breakfast while he looked at the prints on her wall. He had his back to her as she watched his broad shoulders and the flex of his muscles as they moved like the shiver of a horse under his olive skin. His hard buttocks pushed out roundly under the cotton fabric.

She sighed inwardly - this guy was a god! Much as she hated to entertain the idea, she wondered how much she would overlook just in order to keep him. In the back of her mind his reluctance to talk about the fight troubled her. What had he meant when he said that there was more to it than she could know? It did not mean that he was a crook, but her professional instincts were ringing urgent alarm bells.

Too soon she had thrown on her Bench top and jeans and was driving him back to his hotel in her baby Smart sports car. Breakfast had got waylaid when she could no longer bear the temptation of his body and he had decided he could not bear the loneliness of the shower. He collected his bags from the Park Lane Hilton and she gunned it to Heathrow, using everything she had learned as a Class One Metropolitan Police driver.

"Wow! That was like a movie car chase," he exclaimed as she squealed into the Terminal 2 car park.

With ten minutes to spare they arrived at the Departures gate. He took her in his arms and kissed her hungrily yet with a searching vulnerability, asking a deep question as he looked into her eyes. She let herself melt into his arms. Out of the corner of her eye she caught the flash of a camera as the resident Heathrow news hounds heard that Freddie was on their turf.

"To be honest I don't want to go back without you. I have business and a TV interview. I have to go."

She lay her cheek on his chest, "It's only a few days - I'll think of nothing else," she said looking up at him.

With a final wave he strode though the doors and was gone. Probably he was late, but Air France would hold the flight!

Anna let out a sigh. He was a mistaken choice from the menu that might take years off her life, but the taste was delicious. As a young cop she had often asked druggies and gamblers why they didn't just stop doing it. Up to two days ago she had known so little of life.

Back at her flat she called her father.

"Dad."

"Anna - what on earth is going on - you want to come to France with a client?" asked a deep concerned very English well spoken voice.

"It's a guy called Freddie La Salle."

"Yeah - the boxer - met him in Cannes I believe."

"Well, we met in London," she began, pouring out the whole story aside leaving out the extent of their affair, "And all I need is for you to play along with the story that I work for the business."

"So you want me to lie."

"Uh, yes," she replied.

"And if it comes to it will you be cuddling up to him and searching his pockets?"

"I don't think it will come to that - I mean he seems so decent and honest."

"Is that the cop or the lovesick female speaking?" He asked with a note of kindness.

"Who said anything about love?" she half laughed.

"You didn't have to Anna. Look - just get him to Antibes on Friday. I'll trust you to know what you are doing - but truth and love don't always mix - you don't need me to tell you that. Sometimes we cannot express our lives just the way we would like you know."

She imagined him at the other end of the line. His tanned weather-beaten seafaring face and his white hair untidily swept back. It was odd that he had put things in the way that he had.

"I love only you Dad. Trust me and thanks," she answered, sending a big noisy kiss down the receiver and ringing off.

Chapter 6

Someone was knocking the door.

"Is this about God wanting me to change my gas supplier?" she said abruptly looking at a weedy youngish guy in jeans and a worn leather jacket.

"Ms Leyton... um... Inspector... I've got some information for you. Maybe I can help - maybe we can work together. We need to talk."

His voice was London British. She quickly surveyed him - thirty-ish, quick nervous movements. If it came to a fight she could eat him. She relaxed a little. She was a detective and something about this little grungy geeky guy came across to her.

"So - you're press or a private detective right?

"Hey - respect Inspector," replied the little guy with a grin, "Fly Fisher - I reel 'em in."

"What kinda line is that?" she answered with a laugh at her own pun. He nodded an approval of her wit and smiled broadly.

"Okay - that's my column, I'm Pete Making. I'm a reporter on Fan-Tale magazine. I guess you've not heard of us..."

"Right!" she said her mind racing through all possible angles.

"I wanna talk about Freddie La Salle, murder and global match fixing by criminals. Am I getting through?" he asked simply fixing her with keen smiling eyes.

"You got through," she replied opening the door, "any nonsense and you're on the way to jail."

She got them both a coffee. This odd little reporter smiled and filled her in.

"Sport - ya know - it's only the mugs who think it's a game. But gambling ain't even a game - if it was the winners would all be crooks. I'm an investigative journalist. This fight with Brennan is fixed. Your Freddie hasn't even put on a glove for training. Either you're on the case or you're being hoodwinked."

"Okay - but first tell me how you found me."

"I followed you from the restaurant last night. I got a tip from a couple of paps who freelance for us that Freddie was out on the town with a pretty special girl."

Anna frowned with indignation but let it ride in view of the compliment.

"I followed you here from Freddie's restaurant. I saw you clinching on Westminster Bridge. The lady in the salon downstairs whispered to me you were a cop when I told her I was delivering a special bouquet and I had to find you before they wilted."

"You should be a cop."

"Huh - I'm too damn small Anna."

She thought quickly. Probably he didn't know she was on the match fixing operation. He had followed her and got lucky when he learned she was a cop.

"So - you tell me what's going on. The crooks want Freddie to lose the fight I guess cos their money is on Brennan. If Freddie doesn't train then he's gonna lose. So, the odds will be on the other guy to win so the mob gets less money. Surely they want it to look like Freddie will win and sting all the punters who back him," she said, aware that this was the first time she had really thought about the facts.

The weedy guy nodded and looked at her keenly.

"There's a factor X somewhere in Freddie's life Anna. Something out of place. I wanna know if he's in on the deal or if he's on some kinda mission. He's not hiding... maybe that's part of the plan. You must remember that the crooks can play the bookie and punter on the internet. The important thing for them is to know the result. My guess... and it's only a guess, is that Freddie is playing them along. At his last fight they thought it was enough to fix the ref. Everyone in the game knows that Freddie wins on points. This time they won't risk that..."

"And if Brennan wins he's hot property as their champ and great white hope all in one," said Anna.

"You got it... He's a rough house brawler. That's real box office."

"So what's Freddie up to?"

"You tell me Anna. Word is he's out of shape. Freddie is a distance man. He can't reckon on a short fight with a knock down. He just hasn't got that type of punching power... he's not a vicious guy Anna. If he stands against Brennan without training he's gonna get badly hurt," said the reporter with a dispassionate expertise.

"In your view - would they kill Freddie?"

"Too right they would. He knows what happened in Marseille and what happened to the ref. They'll kill anyone in the way. That means you. That means me."

Anna nodded. There were so many risks to weigh up.

"And this factor X... " she began.

"The guy is a mystery to me Anna. I'm impartial but I'm a real fan but I've never seen him open up and go for an opponent, not even when he's hurt. No show boat stuff... just a day at the office. He doesn't do trash."

She thought deeply. Obviously he was on the trail. She could not risk her association with Freddie being known to Scotland Yard at this stage and she could never risk it being known to whoever killed that referee.

"Look - there are problems here for both of us," she began, "let's keep this between ourselves. To be honest I know nothing of this. Freddie is a boyfriend - he has no idea I'm a cop and if you tell him - I've got ways of fixing you up... if you get my meaning Pete?" she half snarled, wanting to be sure that she conveyed a meaningful threat. This little geek could get her killed.

"Anna - Inspector - it will be our secret. I've heard there's a squad on the job. I'll leave it to you to make contact. I'll share what I know in return for the inside story on La Salle - that's all I want."

"I'll do my best. There's twenty six thousand officers in the Met Police. It'll take me a while to get a source. In the meantime give me something you couldn't just know from the papers."

"I'll give you a name," he began nervously, " MauroTondelli - he killed that referee. Tortured him first then strangled him with his bare hands. Threw the body in the river."

Anna nodded. She could check this out.

"Give me a card Pete... I'll call you."

The little guy shook his head.

"No cards Inspector. Who knows whose hands you could fall into? Get your cell phone and dial the number I give you. That way we know each other. Don't put any tag on that number. I'll do the same."

This guy was no mug. She dialed the number he gave her. She heard the phone ring in his pocket.

"Stay in touch Anna - feel free to call me. I'll trust you to contact me."

With that he stood up, offered a surprisingly firm handshake and headed for the door.

She sat down wearily and considered her options. This case was heating up. And just what was the factor X in Freddie's life?

Chapter 7

A few hours later she arrived at Judy's rambling old three storey town house near Hammersmith Broadway. She had to talk to someone or she would burst. Perhaps she needed someone to calm her down and get her back on the rails. She also needed an action plan for the week ahead, best discussed away from the office. Judy had been delighted with the chance of a girlie chat.

"Fizzio-therapy," she announced as she plonked down two bottles of sparkling Pinot Grigio.

Judy held her son Zak in her arms in the centre of the toy strewn lounge. The three year old Mia ran to Anna exclaiming over and over "

"There's Nobolins in the forest. Nobolins! Nobolins!"

"Nobolins?" Anna repeated.

"Goblins," laughed Judy.

Anna sat down while Mia presented the evidence for nobolins in the shape of a big story book.

"You're a natural," commented Judy.

Anna thought seriously for a few seconds. Sure she was off the pill but just at the start of her cycle. She knew that as a boxer Freddie would be checked out but she was living dangerously for sure. Just now there were other problems.

She watched her friend mothering the children, unable to reconcile the picture with the tough demon driver cop from their days at Brixton. Once the kids were in bed they opened the wine and Anna opened her heart.

"Plan A is a transfer to the underwater search squad, a check at the clinic and a morning after pill," announced Judy when she had finished.

Anna laughed, "Is there a plan B?"

"Plan B is to get you to France next week for a bang on the boat. We do not tell Beaumont that you are shagging the suspect and are so loved up that your knees don't work."

"Loved up - is it obvious?"

"Yeah - like a big zit on your nose baby!"

Anna smiled at Judy's wonderful way with words. Her friend continued.

"So - Monday morning conference I'll get a keen young detective from Criminal Intelligence to bring up the story from Interpol about Freddie boy. It's best if I don't look involved cos you're the witch and I'm the cat as far as our dear commander is concerned. Then you can jump in saying - "What a coincidence... this guy is a client of my father and he's gonna be in the South of France." Then you offer to pop down and check him out."

"It's risky, but I'll go for it - we never worried about risks in the past did we?"

"We were dumb street cops Anna, just kids - shall we open the other bottle?" Judy laughed, - "but I'll tell you one thing - that Beaumont Locke is a real premiership slime bag."

"Destined for commissioner," added Anna.

"Commissioner?" echoed Brian's voice swerving through the toys in his uniform and stab vest, "it's a kind offer but I'm busy."

"Good shift?" asked Judy, kissing her husband's balding head.

"I'm still alive, no one else died," he answered wearily.

Anna smiled. She liked Brian and would have trusted him with anything. He was going nowhere in the police but he was worth ten of Commander Locke.

"Brian - you know of Freddie La Salle?" prompted Judy.

"Sure - he's a legend. He's about to fight Brennan in New York. Rather him than me. Brennan is great white hope and great white shark all in one. Never been defeated, never gone the distance. Fearsome puncher - know what I mean like a psycho savage? La Salle is a gent - goes in there to beat the guy, not beat him up."

"So who will win?" asked Anna anxiously.

"La Salle has the class. He always goes the distance, never throws the big punches. If the ref lets Brennan fight the whole match with his head in Freddie's face then I think La Salle will get nailed. Brennan is the home town boy. La Salle must need the cash - this fight is huge box office."

Anna winced at the thought of Freddie unconscious on the floor with the crowd baying for his blood. He didn't seem to need the money.

"What's this fight worth to the winner?" she asked.

"Prize money - perhaps a million dollars. TV and the rest about 20 million."

"I might be tempted myself," commented Anna.

"Not if you'd seen Brennan in full psycho attack," Pete chuckled.

"Never mind - you are only risking your career, your health and the trust of your family Anna," said Judy concernedly.

Anna nodded, "I know - and it's fantastic."

Chapter 8

Once back to her flat she lay gratefully in bed. Loneliness ached inside that only one man could soothe. Her mobile was ringing and she fumbled to find it.

"Anna?"

She almost kissed the phone. It was him!

"I had to call - it's late chérie - I'm sorry."

"No - don't be sorry..."

"I was thinking of you - you know, how it was last night."

She thought of his face, his big strong hand holding the phone.

"Me too - how's Paris?"

"Oh - I had to do that TV show - just a dumb interview about boxing. I'm at home now, looking out of the window onto the Boulevard St Michel. My city is very beautiful too," he purred in his soft French accent.

"Freddie - I wish..."

"I wish it too ma belle - how I wish..."

"If only I could kiss you - if only I could hold you," she almost cried with frustration.

"Our time will come - once this whole business is over I'll be free."

"What business?"

"The fight and all the stuff that goes with it," he sighed wearily, "I want another life now but I have to focus in."

"I was thinking... you know perhaps you could get injured in training or something like that..."

He chuckled, "Yes - you are thinking like a woman who wants to keep her baby at home on the first day at school. There is more to this show than a sweet girl can imagine. It's not like the boat business mon amour."

She swallowed a surge of anger. She didn't sell bloody boats! She knew more of this tough world that he could imagine. How she longed to open her own heart, but since she had lied to him she could hardly blame him for believing her... but what was it he had called her? Mon amour?

"Mon amour? Mon amour?" she echoed back at him.

"OK - that slipped out, it's a lovely word. I was not expecting you in my life right now - or ever I guess," he said in a slow husky voice.

"I understand... I feel... it is all so fast," she began, battling with her raging emotions of desire and frustratio, "Can I meet you in Antibes on Thursday afternoon? I'll call you as soon as I have all the details."

"I'll pick you up from the airport in Nice."

"There's no need,"

"There's every need Anna - every need in the whole world. In a few days I fly to the States for training camp - I might as well be going to the moon. I mean Anna... Anna, it is so good to say your name - couldn't you come to Paris?"

Every cell in her body craved and ached for him. If only she could be with him NOW!

She was out of control and reckless. Probably he would think she was a wicked girl. Maybe he knew he was in danger. She could just pretend to herself she was on his case. For sure there were crooks in the soup and with luck she could clean up the bowl and leave him aside. If the worst came to the worst she would just disappear and get on a plane.

"Yes - I'll come," she replied, wondering how she could possibly swing it.

"When?" he questioned, with a note of joy in his voice that thrilled her.

"Tomorrow night - a late plane into Paris Charles de Gaulle."

"No boats to sell in London?"

Her heart was pounding. He could not imagine the hoops she was going to have to jump through. If only she were a Daddy's girl who sold the odd boat.

"The rain stopped - the ark business is history."

"Anna," he exclaimed suddenly, "this is crazy - but I don't want to stop."

How he wanted her. He needed a girl at his side but that was just how it had started. Now things were different but he could never explain that now. Probably he would never be able to tell her.

"I'll let you know my flight," she said, softly kissing the phone.

"Until tomorrow," he whispered.

Her mind swam with both joy and worry. Once again she had acted spontaneously with no idea of how to pull off such a trip. Suddenly her mind swapped back to that time before when she had just acted out of passion. It was a flaw in her nature and maybe she would have to pay for it again. She thought of holding him, the touch of his lips, his strong wide shoulders that filled her with desire and a sense of being protected. These few days now could be her entire life and there would be no regrets. She hugged the pillow and said his name over and over. Soon enough it would be another week and she would have to dig even deeper into the delicious hole that was beginning to swallow her.

Chapter 9

The Monday morning conference came to order with Beaumont Locke performing his self important stand up and sit down ritual. A new face was at the table. Anna smiled as she recognized Deputy Assistant Commissioner Christine Jones who had overall command of the Interpol London bureau. She outranked Beaumont and both women knew each other from the streets of South London. She was in her fifties, handsome with cropped hair in a professional black pinstripe trouser suit, crisp white shirt and rugby club tie complete with red floppy hanky. She smiled at Anna with warmth that she knew was not entirely without meaning. She herself had chosen a plain deep cream suit, stockings and high heels. Her lips were deep red and her raven hair shone as it fell onto her shoulders. She had half expected to see Christine at the meeting and in view of her audacious plan had dressed to impress.

Judy moved to Anna's side.

"The NCIS guy just lapped it all up and has done some research of his own. There's money pouring on Freddie to lose," she explained.

"But why can't he win - he's the world champion after all?"

"Because Brennan's in his own back yard and the judges score the fight. In the States the most aggressive fighter can win even if he scores fewer points. Perhaps Freddie is in bed with these guys - but if he is why the hell is he swanning about trying to look like a loser. He needs to look like a winner but lose. The possibilities are infinite," said Judy with a shrug.

"Freddie must know all this. Just why the hell is he taking this fight?" asked Anna, mainly to herself.

"That's what you are going to find out honey," said Judy, patting her arm.

The young detective gave a detailed briefing. It seemed bizarre to hear Freddie talked about as a suspect or at least an object of enquiry in a police case. The speaker did a brilliant job, making Freddie look like the key to the whole business and showing himself as a gifted crime analyst, enjoying his chance to shine in front of many possible patrons.

Anna's heart was racing, her mouth dry. She just had to stay calm to pull off this deal. The speaker brought his report to an end with the words:

"Everything points to this forthcoming fight being manipulated by a group of New York criminals. Without inside information we cannot know if La Salle or Brennan are in on the deal, but Brennan is more or less owned by the good old traditional Mafia. As world champion he would be worth a huge amount of cash for future fights and the scrap with La Salle is worth forty million dollars in gambling alone. All the money is on Brennan to win but the odds now are just for Schmucks. All the serious bets went on at 20 to 1. Freddie is driving the odds on Brennan down... so crooks won't be too pleased with him I suspect. A real gambler would back Freddie... but a guy out of training with a girl on each arm...well, that is a gamble."

"Do we know who killed the referee?"asked Anna casually, reflecting she ought to know more about gambling.

An FBI analyst stood to answer.

"We can't prove a thing but we do have information from a Jersey cab driver that a hood called Tondelli used his garage to torture him before killing him. No one outside the police knows this as far as we know."

Anna nodded her thanks. At least the geek was up to speed. There was a short silence, broken by Christine Jones.

"Great - so we have a foot on the ladder. We can get the FBI on Brennan. As for La Salle, his last fight was surrounded by suspicion wasn't it?" she asked.

"So, we need an operation to look at La Salle," said Beaumont Locke.

Anna took a deep breath and tried to suppress the adrenalin pumping into her blood.

"I may be able to help. La Salle is a client of my father. I believe I can get a good insight into him," she said, hoping she sounded calm.

Commander Locke leaned back in his chair and looked at her. With a show of arrogance he linked his hands behind his head.

"Whoa! This is fantasy island stuff. You are an Interpol officer Inspector. Your job is liaison and issues of language and cooperation. There's no way you can wander off on some kind of maverick mission."

Anna swallowed her anger and glanced at Christine Jones, who smiled and almost winked.

"You have a better approach Commander Locke?" she asked coldly.

He snapped forward and spoke angril, "I have no approach - this is the first I've heard of La Salle!"

"Perhaps you should keep up to date. Evidently Anna has taken the trouble to stay on top of the game," she said with a frigid smile.

"That is neither here nor there. If we need to look at La Salle, the bloody French can do it. It is not Inspector Leyton's job," he spat angrily.

"As head of the Interpol Bureau I believe I may assign my own staff," replied Christine with a menacing tweak of her eyebrow, "perhaps Anna can tell us the whole story?"

Christine beamed at Anna and signaled for her to begin. Suddenly Beaumont banged the table.

"Who is chair of this meeting? I will not have Interpol trying to grab the limelight from all these other departments," he thundered pompously.

"So we'll just ignore Anna's contribution shall we? Perhaps when the Olympics come to London in 2012 we'll get another chance. I wouldn't want to be telling the Home Secretary that we let our little squabbles prevent us from locking up these crooks."

Anna watched him subside. This was the kind of politics that he could not risk on his way up. Christine Jones had the ear of the Home Office and had friends in government.

She steadied her nerves and began to speak.

"Freddie La Salle is looking to buy an exclusive motor - cruiser from Leyton Marine. He is due to try out a boat in Antibes on Friday and is meeting a salesperson in Paris tomorrow morning."

"And you are telling us that Daddy's perfect pet is going to snuggle up to him and induce him to tell all with one sweep of your lashes Inspector," sneered Beaumont.

Despite the tense situation the notion of snuggling up to Freddie helped her relax.

"Why not? I've done plenty of undercover and surveillance work," she fired back.

"So this fighter, this thug is just going to roll over is he? These sporty celebs have trashy tarts at every turn..."

"Freddie is a cultured man and well known art collector," she retorted.

"Ooh - you can look at his brushstrokes," he mocked with a false guffaw.

"This is not a personal matter Commander. These sexist and derogatory remarks could be career threatening," warned Christine Jones, fixing him with an icy stare.

Around the table junior officers glanced at one another and shuffled their papers awkwardly. It was rare to be party to this kind of jousting. Anna winced inwardly, ashamed that she had used deceit to manipulate this conflict in order to fulfill her selfish desire. She comforted herself with the belief that she could provide good intelligence for the squad.

"I'm quite happy to agree to this mission - that is if Commander Locke has no further objections. This is your enquiry and I would so hate to interfere," announced Christine imperiously.

He narrowed his eyes and looked at her. His face was white with anger.

"She is your baby just as long as you take responsibility. You know that this is completely outside the brief of an Interpol officer."

"Her brief is as I define it," she replied with a thin cold steel blade of a smile.

The meeting resumed with a couple of routine reports and drew to a close. Anna bundled up her files and scampered to her office with Judy. As soon as the door was closed she slumped down and let out a long, "Sheesh!"

"God - that was dinosaur stuff in there - great beasts battling it out in the political swamp. Beaumont isn't half the man she is! You'd better watch out. I think she's got the hots for you, unless you fancy a walk on the wild side," warned Judy.

Anna giggled, relieved it was over, "That's the last thing I want."

"You caught me off balance in there. Why go to Paris today?"

"He phoned last night."

"And?" Judy questioned.

"Judy, I just want him so much!"

"So, it is to be a shagathon in gay 'Paree' Inspector," boomed Judy, mocking Beaumont's sarcastic tone, "and just what is French for pillow talk?"

"Les confidences sur l'oreiller," Anna replied.

"Smart Bitch!" quipped Judy, "it's not the dreaded L word is it?"

"It's the A word," laughed Anna.

"A word, what's the A word - Aardvark?"

"Amour - Amour," Anna enthused, reliving the word on his lips, the word pumping down the phone line, reliving the tingle of his touch, his hardness, his male scent.

"Just look at you for Pete's sake," said Judy, jolting her back to the present, "you're loved up to the back teeth. Just watch out. The guy is a bull elephant and is probably a crook. If this goes wrong our beloved commander will strip you off and peg you out for the crows. Haven't you had enough trouble for a while Anna?"

"I know. I'm misleading everyone but I just can't help it," she replied seriously. Judy reached across the desk and squeezed her hand.

"If you love him then that's reason enough," she said calmly.

"Do you believe that? This isn't some soft romance novel Judy. Is love a big enough reason?"

"It is the reason Anna. Love is when they give you a free pass just as long as you're prepared to pay any price."

"You're a real diamond Judy," replied Anna, taking her friend's comment as a blessing. Already she had her cell phone in her hand and was texting Freddie as Christine Jones breezed in to the office.

"You guys free for lunch?"

"Ma'am - I've gotta get down to Sainsbury's - Little Mia has a party and... "

"Oh the joys of motherhood, I was far more hood than mother," said Christine wearily, "always figured this rotten world didn't need any more of my weird genes."

"Never quite saw it like that," replied Judy, a little taken aback.

"Thank goodness... anyway - Anna you can join an old girl surely?"

Anna smiled warmly. Christine Jones was a police icon. With her brilliant legal mind she was a qualified barrister. Anna had first met her when she was a Detective Superintendent at Streatham. Having already been voted by street cops the man you most wanted on your side in a fight, criminals awarded her awarded the nickname of 'The Blue Witch'.

Now she was in her last couple of years and could have already retired to a cottage. She was stocky without being overweight and her face was untouched by makeup. Her only ornamentation was a gent's wristwatch with a broad brown leather strap.

Anna fell in by her side.

"There's a new Italiano across the river - you can show off your language skills. How lovely and talented you are Anna - it will be wonderful. They have all those confused waiter boys with tight little bottoms."

Anna could see a wry smile on Judy's face. She admired Christine professionally but had no doubt as to her outrageous personal character. Her intervention at the meeting had been fantastic and she regretted how she had deceived her. She didn't want to undermine any future trust between them, let alone any career implications.

"Let's walk and have a chat about your mission - and I'll get a couple of smokes on the way," prompted Christine, taking her arm.

Looking at her, Anna found a warmth and compassion in her eyes that was not entirely unpleasant. Within herself she was beginning to discover a calculating deviousness that she didn't like, but which gave her a sense of power that almost thrilled her. In contrast with this moment, her time with Freddie left her powerless and swept away on a wave of desire. She smiled at Christine, wondering what she knew of helpless love and the shortness of life and its seasons.

The day was bright, slightly autumnal. The sunlight shone through the polished luster of her hair. Her red lips added a tantalizing sensual splash to her beauty.

"You're a lovely talented young woman," declared Christine as if to a thoroughbred filly as she powered across Vauxhall Bridge, "you have a wonderful career ahead."

Anna desperately tried to keep up in her high heels which were no match for the older woman's burnished black brogues.

"Thank you Ma'am," said Anna.

"Stop that bullshit... to you I'm Chris," she ordered, taking a deep pull on her second Marlboro.

"And thanks for your help this morning at the meeting."

"No worries - that Beaumont is such a pompous ass. I first met him when he was a bobby at Tottenham. Absolute jargon and paperwork jockey - very modern. They used to call him the Olympic torch - because he never went out," she laughed, "Wasn't there some kind of thing between you two?"

"There was - I was foolish but I've learned from the mistake believe me. I didn't know what I was or what I wanted."

"And do you know now?"

"I'm beginning to see I think," replied Anna with a deliberate note of ambiguity, sensing just a little of her power and letting her eyes stay on Christine's face.

"Just be careful with that La Salle. He's a bit of a charmer and Interpol has not issued chastity belts since the crusades," warned Christine.

"I've never met him - I'm only going to pose as the boss's daughter and try to sell him a boat."

"Be careful my dear. We all felt for you after the crash - but you are damaged - you need time to repair."

They reached the restaurant in Strutton Ground, just a short trot from Scotland Yard and took a pavement table. Chris ordered a meat feast pizza and a large lager. Anna went for a Mozzarella salad and a bottle of mineral water.

"I want you to find out who contacts La Salle and who he contacts. Does he want to win this fight? He's been wandering about in London, so he's obviously not in training. Then there's Mom - she's hauled herself up from trailer trash to loadsa cash and looks like one tough cookie."

"What do you know about Mom?" asked Anna, trying to sound professional.

"Just what I read when Beaumont was droning on. Looks like she met Monsieur La Salle when she was a student at the Sorbonne. She's from a poor but aspirational family who turned their back on her when she married this French poet hippy and ended up with a baby. I guess the marriage didn't work out and she ends up back in the States."

"Quite a story," commented Anna.

"The story we want is some evidence on these hoods that are muscling in on sport. These gambling scams can wreck the credibility of sport all together. If these guys are still running around when the Olympics come to London, our political masters will not be amused. To be frank my sweet gal - I don't care how we get our evidence," said Christine flatly as if she were talking about a trip to the seaside.

"I'll do my best," nodded Anna, beginning to feel the weight of what she had undertaken.

"You can go to the top from this case but don't think this is a walk in the park. This fight is in New York and our old Mafia friends will be in the shadows. You'll be undercover without a safety net. They've already killed and some odd girlfriend could get caught in the crossfire. We're talking millions and millions of dollars, pounds, euro and yen."

Anna looked into the other woman's eyes. She had nerves of steel and had seen it all.

"Report in as and how you can but don't compromise your role. You'll be out there alone. Provided your cover is intact, you shouldn't be at risk," added Christine, calling the waiter and paying with a large tip, waving away change. "When you get back we must have a chat about your future and how you could develop."

"That would be nice - I wouldn't want any favors Chris," replied Anna, feeling very aware of herself.

"Who said anything about favors? You are very special you know. Advice and friendship is all I can offer. Now I must dash. Meeting at the Yard on Terrorism and then the BBC want an interview on sex trade trafficking from Asia."

As they parted, Anna was surprised to find herself embraced by her superior. Standing cheek to cheek she let herself soften a little, as Christine held her slightly too firmly.

"Sisters are doing it for themselves you know - we can really crack this case," said Chris. Anna returned her embrace for a second and then stepped back.

Christine took a business card from her pocket and handed it to her, "This is my personal mobile. Never give it to anyone else or tell anyone that you know it. If ever you need to talk personally or need help never hesitate."

Anna thanked her, watching her light a cigarette and stride away towards Victoria Street on her way to her meeting at the Yard. Now that she had gone she felt a surge of warmth and emotion for the woman. She was a brilliantly talented but unfulfilled human being. Just a few days ago Anna would never have been able to know the burden of Love by its absence. What longings lay buried in the heart of Deputy Assistant Commissioner Christine Jones, she could only guess. Now she must turn to her own quest and follow it through regardless of cost.

Chapter 10

"What should I take to wear?" she asked Judy excitedly when she got back to the office.

"Will you be out on the boat?"

"Of course, I'll need to be sexy and smart for Paris."

Her mind swam with all the conflicting aspects of the next few days. The thought of his body, the scent of his skin, his broad massive shoulders filled her. How to uncover his contacts? Could she just take his mobile? Would she be able to betray him - the only man who had ever made her feel this way - the only man she had ever loved?

The desk phone was ringing. Judy mimed that it was Beaumont and hung up.

"His master's voice - he wants to see you," she said with a weak grin.

"Deep joy," said Anna. She was not surprised and he would be smarting after the meeting. Nothing he could do or say could stop her now. She threw back her head and walked down the corridor.

"Sit down Inspector," he sneered with a languid flourish of his hand towards a chair in front of his oversized executive desk. He had always rejected issue furniture and moved around with his own fittings.

"Quite a little triumph this morning," he continued.

"Let's just get on shall we," she hissed.

"Ah, yes forgive me. Let us do just that."

His words slithered out like snakes as he opened a desk drawer and tossed a copy of the Evening Standard at her, "Page seven - the London Ear gossip column."

"Is this a game?" she asked angrily.

"That's what I want to know Anna..."

Anna flicked through the pages. Her eyes fell on a photo of Freddie outside his Chelsea restaurant. The girl by his side was partly hidden by a chance swirl of dark hair across her face.

Her heart leapt. She had been in some tight spots and she had to keep her nerve.

"So - he's got a girlfriend," she shrugged.

"Girlfriend!" he exploded, "girlfriend! Do you think I don't know who that is?"

She stared back at him. The gloves were off and she had nothing to lose.

"So what are you going to do?"

"I'll start by making a call to your mistress and champion Christine Jones."

"Will you - and say what? Tell her that Freddie has a girl?"

"Tell her that her little favorite is a lying conniving bitch who set up an intelligence briefing so that she could shag some thug in the South of France at the taxpayer's expense," he thundered.

"Are you saying I can't do a professional job on La Salle?" she retorted.

"I'm sure you're a pro in the bedroom!"

"Look Beaumont - let's keep to business. If you think you can prove that's my photo you had better go ahead. Christine Jones may not care - she might think I'm a hero for getting so deep undercover - except it's not me! And believe me mister - I'll deny it. I've never revealed how you scrambled away from me when you thought I could go to jail. If you interfere with me I'll make sure your name stinks."

"How dare you speak to me like that Inspector? You will address me as your superior officer."

"I'll make your name stink Sir!" she shouted.

He stood up and paced the room,"I can convince anyone that it is you," he fumed.

"And look like a small man with a big grudge. You need this squad to succeed as much as anyone. Nelson put his telescope to his blind eye and went on to be a national hero. There's a spare plinth in Trafalgar Square for you Beaumont," she said, watching him calculating and weighing up his options and how it could affect his career. No one on the way up could risk any sort of trouble. "You engineered my placement on this squad to keep your influence over me. Any hint of harassment or abuse of power and you're finished," she continued, beginning to relax as she saw her words cutting in to him. In truth she had no desire to ruin him. She had used him in the same way that he had used her. He knew she could very possibly get some evidence to swing this case and no one would thank him for spoiling the opportunity. There was nothing for him to gain and whether or not she was Freddie's lover made no professional difference.

He stood motionless looking out of the window.

"Just get out Anna - just get out! This conversation never happened."

She thought for as moment. He was still dangerous. He could give an anonymous tip off either inside the police or outside. She was going to get close to some pretty ruthless characters and had no desire to die just yet.

"If ever I thought you'd exposed me, I'll finish you Beaumont - you know that don't you," she said icily, looking directly into his eyes.

"Deep down you're a ruthless selfish bitch Anna."

"I try Sir. I really do try," she replied almost smiling.

"I told you to get out!" he hissed with a strangled anger.

She turned and walked calmly from the room to her own office. She'd trodden on some thin ice in her time… and one day it would give beneath her feet. She had been dishonest and devious. Everything she had achieved for herself was on the line. If she used Freddie to full advantage it could slingshot her career to the top. But then the thought of his name made her repeat it over and over as if he were holding her and she was kissing him. She cupped her face in her hands as she remembered his kind intelligent eyes, the touch of his powerful hands.

"Hey - what's up?" Judy asked.

"You startled me - you should have gone home."

"I've been getting your briefing file together - it looks like you had a pretty torrid interview."

"I'm in the Standard with Freddie - we were snapped at his restaurant, but you can't see my face. Beaumont knows but I've convinced him to keep his trap shut."

"I've loaded everything onto your laptop. There's a blank SIM card in the carry case for copying the files off his mobile. The FBI is interested in a mob lawyer called Gino Scapaticci. He's believed to be masterminding the gambling and is also Brennan's business manager. He has booked a flight to Nice, landing on Wednesday. It might just be coincidence that Freddie will be in the area, but come on… "

"How would some mobster know what Freddie was doing - unless from the man himself - or Mom?" Anna queried thinking out loud.

"Quite so my dear Watson," said Judy, "it may be nothing in itself but it makes me wonder about your man."

She stifled an impulse to defend him, but being in love with him did not mean he was innocent.

"I do have an open mind," she assured her friend.

"Open mind - open every bloody thing. I still remember passion before it got thrown out with the cold supermarket value beans and the disposable nappies," laughed Judy.

Anna hugged her out of affection and gratitude for all she had done to help her. Butterflies rioted in her stomach at the thought that she would soon be with him.

"Just watch out mate," warned Judy.

Anna grabbed her laptop and headed for the door. She had a plane to catch.

Chapter 11

She was anything but frilly, yet this trip posed a wardrobe nightmare. She had to fly to Paris and spend at least a day and an evening there. Then she had to travel to the South of France, go out on a sea trial and spend a couple of evenings at dinner. In the end she took deck shoes, culottes and some T shirts. She chose the regulation black number, a deep blue strapless knee length dress, a dark red satin blouse and black mini skirt and a beaded oyster top and matching trousers. For good measure she threw in her black wrap, her faithful leather jacket and a smart fitted blazer. For general wear she took some Dolce and Gabbana hipster jeans, six pairs of shoes, the whole drawer of underwear and two silk night dresses. To travel she wore her Abercrombie hoodie and Levi jeans with ankle boots. With the suitcase forced shut she phoned the mini cab and swerved to Heathrow, texting Freddie with flight details.

She grabbed a coffee at Starbucks and glanced at the Sky News screen as she waited to board. Nothing mattered that this world could throw up - nothing. A face on the screen, half familiar, a line of text running below... Sports Journalist Peter Making found dead, police seeking information...

Anna sighed resignedly. Her number would be on his phone with the time of the call. She had decided to say nothing and now she was half in a frame. She should have told Judy but it was too late now. If Making had followed her to her flat then perhaps the killer had been on the same trail.

Even so she was alive... and she wanted to live. For now she was a girl who sold boats.

Twenty minutes after Air France 2271 had screeched from the dark night sky into Paris Charles De Gaulle she half ran through the doors into the arrivals hall. And there he was - tall, broad, tight muscled strong and handsome! His dark cropped hair adding to his air of toughness belied by his soft brown eyes. He wore a battered leather flight jacket, white T shirt, faded jeans and burnished brown leather chisel toed shoes. He looked delicious, ruthless, compassionate, sexy and hers!

Despite all her instructions to herself to stay dignified and cool, on impulse she found herself running towards him, towing her heavy wheeled case. He caught her and swept her up in his arms. Again she felt his overwhelming strength as he held her cradled her like a baby. The hard warm living steel of his body thrilled her, just as the tender gentleness of his searching kiss drained her of all resistance. He was holding her and she was his! There was nothing else in the world.

"Merci - for having come for me," she gasped.

"Nothing could have stopped me Chérie," he said in his deep voice.

He took her bag as they walked to his car, his arm around her shoulder and his large hand spread down enough onto her chest to slightly raise her breast and increase her awareness of her nipple. Already she was longing for his touch, physically responding to him. She slipped into the car - a silver Mercedes CLS 500. As he leaned across and kissed her cheek she ran her fingers back through his hair and breathed in his cologne and potent male scent. She folded her fingers around his neck, feeling his bull strength. He raised his hand to her cheek and through her hair. The thrill of his touch sent jolts of excitement sparking through her flesh, tingling in her breasts and the apex of her thighs. She pulled him towards her, wanting him inside, knowing that she would come if he just touched her. He was total male and she was woman.

"This is so wonderful and so crazy," she whispered

"Anna - the other night - things just happened. It was so overwhelming. It was as if everything had led me to you," he replied, bathing her soul in the warm sweeping torrent of his dark eyes.

"This is supposed to be a business trip," she laughed.

"And so it is. It entirely our own business - and I do want a boat," he beamed.

"Of course," she sighed, settling back into the soft leather as he nudged the powerful Mercedes out of the airport and into the tumble and jumble of le Boulevard Périphérique.

It had been quite a day and now she could relax. She enjoyed the silent surging push of the Mercedes but was slightly surprised by his choice of such a businessman's car.

"I thought maybe you would have a Ferrari," she commented.

"When I won the world title I bought one - and every punk wanted to race the champ. One day I dreamed I would meet the most beautiful raven haired woman and I would want to hear what she said."

Anna smiled. So he was a smooth operator. Tomorrow could be police work but tonight she was in Paris with the man who had brought her back to life and who had opened her heart.

"You're not just a pretty face are you Freddie."

"The pretty face is your job in this team."

They began to slide into the centre of Paris. She recognized le Quai de la Rapée and le Pont d'Austerlitz as the road slipped past. The River Seine and its bridges were rendered magical by lights. She watched his strong hands on the wheel, longing for the moment when they could touch properly. He eased into a private underground garage.

"Voilà - Boulevard St. Michel," he said with a gentle smile.

They took the lift to his fifth floor penthouse. As the heavy paneled door opened she saw into a huge lounge, one wall of which was filled with leather bound books. An enormous French window opened out onto a balcony looking out over the rooftops of Paris to the Seine. Freddie faded up the mellow wall lights allowing her to see the sumptuous blue carpet and what looked like an original Renoir hanging over an ornate Louis XV fireplace. Antique chairs, clocks and ornaments were tastefully displayed around the room. A large gilt framed mirror reflected a magnificent chandelier hanging from the ceiling.

"It's so, so lovely," she sighed as he closed the door behind her with a heavy quality laden click.

She turned to him as he came to her, feeling his strong arms possess and caress her. Her knees physically buckled. She kissed him deeply, her tongue searching shamelessly for his. As he responded she could feel him hardening against her belly. She curled her leg behind his and pressed her longing secret lips against his tight rippled thigh.

He eased his head back and looked at her.

"You are so beautiful Anna - I can't believe this cruel world has allowed me to find you."

She lay her head on the contoured bulge of his pecs as he stroked her hair.

"Champagne?" he asked, "this is Paris and it is from my own vineyard... you can't say no."

"I'd love it - but can I get out of these old London and airplane clothes?"

He let her go and she dived into the en suite power shower. She was pleased to see that all the materials were absolutely male. The water revived and enlivened her as it cascaded onto her aroused breasts. She reached down, only too aware of the pleasure of her own touch. She stepped out, spotting a white silk dressing gown on the heated towel rail. She put it on, immediately jolted by his scent and presence. Across the back spread the logo 'Lonsdale' and the words 'Le Professeur - Champion du Monde'. She pulled it around her, thrilling to its aromatic attraction. She pulled up the hood and breathed in his pure clean yet animal scent. Wrapping it around her she walked back into the lounge, making her own show of jabbing and punching like a boxer getting in to the ring.

Freddie was standing at the window. He saw her reflection and turned to her with a broad adoring smile.

"Wow - you look fantastic," he said, smiling and handing her a crystal fluted glass of champagne from the table.

"I love this gown - it smells of you."

"Yeah - sweat blood and tears my love... I wore it at my last fight - you keep it, I could never make it look so good."

"Then you've lost it baby," she squealed,"I'll never give it back."

"Perhaps I'll have to keep you on," he said with a soft smile, "here's to everything that lies ahead".

They touched glasses and drank.

"God! That's good!" she said.

"Vintage Chateau La Salle - just for the boss and his lady," he smiled.

The delicious anticipation of his touch sent seismic thrilling waves through her body. She stood at his side at the window, fighting to maintain a veneer of sophistication. She finished her drink and he stepped back to the bottle and poured them both another. She drank quickly - too quickly - she knew, feeling a glow as her inhibitions burned away like mist in the morning sun. He had come to stand behind her. She felt him rock hard and urgent against her lower back. A jolt of pleasure rocked her as his lips and the teasing lick of his tongue found her neck and his teeth nibbled at her skin. One hand cupped her breast and gently brushed her nipple. She groaned and leaned back against him as his other hand ran down across her belly into the furrow of her moist core. Slowly he began to massage her inner lips against her firm little button, circling lightly yet more and more urgently. Still he licked her neck in the same rhythm as his other hand matched the pulse of her passion as he gently stroked her nipple. The three pulses of lust began to overwhelm her and at first she tried to hold back as she felt her orgasm building and piling like thunder clouds against a pure blue sky on a summer's day.

"Freddie - what are you doing to me - I can't hold back."

"Let go my angel," he whispered huskily, "be a woman for me - be my woman ma belle."

Spasms of joy rushed through her as she let go, sensing his need for her to abandon herself totally to him. Beyond her the Parisian night blended into her consciousness and her surrender to pleasure. He held her as she tilted up her lips to his and kissed him in shudders of ecstasy.

"My sweet baby, my sweet soft baby," he murmured as she grunted out his name in a blur of love and animal passion.

As she subsided for a moment she turned to face him, kissing him deeply. His desire for her was by now all consuming and he felt a desperation for his own release. A trace of her woman scent gripped his senses. He lifted her in his steel arms as if she had no weight, finding her lips with his. She felt herself carried to a huge antique four poster bed. He gasped at her beauty. Her black hair spread carelessly on the cream satin pillow. He feasted his eyes on the supple softness of her body, quickly removing his clothes and lying alongside her, moving his mouth to her breast and his hand to her gorgeous wet soft valley. The feel of her thrilled him as she opened herself to his touch.

She reached out to him. He was hard and massive and twitched as her hand slowly drew him back to reveal his longing flesh. He groaned but fought to hold back. He wanted to plunge into her haven of warm giving love - for his love for her to unite with her body. His finger slipped gently into her as he turned to move above her. She still held him as he found her entrance and felt the parting of her delicious flooding lips. At last he slid into her, pushing to the limit of her soft depths.

She sighed as his power, length and thickness filled and possessed her. He nudged at the roof of her being somewhere deep in her spirit. Some beast had been released from captivity as his movements touched switches of pleasure and lust. She gripped his buttocks, thrilling at their relentless steel tension. She began to buck upwards in ecstasy as waves of uncontrolled shudders swept through her. She let out some animal sound as she saw his broad shoulders above her and gasped in the scent of his male body musk.

He felt the pulsating grip of her joy beneath him as he moved slowly inside her soft soaking body. The awareness of his power over her pumped him harder and harder as he began to climb towards the top of an irresistible slope.

She sensed his growing need and the tension excited her beyond control. As he pressed his lips to her neck groaning "mon amour - mon amour," she trembled against him as surges of orgasm seemed to drench her into senselessness.

And now he had reached the summit of his climb. He bit tenderly at her neck tasting her flesh and her sweat. He began to let himself go, feeling the longing sweet agony of need to release. He was gripping her and filling her and she was holding him, pulling him in deeply, pulling in the male of him to her sweet female love flower.

She felt the ecstatic squeezing and pumping of his muscles inside and outside of her as his seed flowed and jetted into her hot molten core, mixing with her own pulsing jolts of their shared climax. He heard her helpless cry as he groaned her name and gave up control to the power of love and the passion of beasts.

She felt his weight as he subsided onto her breasts. Still he was inside her with the last aftershocks of his release still shuddering through him, as if he were a great tree crashed across her as the storm finally passed. Their bodies were damp with sweat and lust. Their scent and fluids mixed into mellowness in the pale thin light of the room. He was the first to speak.

"Anna - my love - there is no other woman like you - I just lose myself in you."

He lay on his back and she turned on her side placing her leg between his.

"You are my man Freddie. I'm out of control too with all this but I can't stop," she said seriously.

"I never want you to stop... but maybe one day you will wake up and see that you don't know me..."

"I know enough - no one can ever know everything," she said calmly.

She rested her head on his chest as he stroked her hair. Idly she ran her hand over the ridged iron six pack of his stomach muscles. He was beautiful - more beautiful than anything she could ever have imagined. His olive skin was like silk and smelled of male mixed with summer sun and sex.

With an athletic swivel he lay her over on her side and spooned into her back, whispering butterfly kisses onto her shoulders.

"You are my baby for ever - my angel," he murmured as they drifted into warm cuddled sleep.

Chapter 12

When she awoke it was dawn across the city. The distant foreign sound of an ambulance siren echoing from the Seine reminded her where she was. She ran her foot up and down his muscular calf. A question formed in her mind and escaped before she measured its weight.

"Why are you a boxer - you are a cultured man?"

"It is a noble art," he murmured.

"You know that's a cliché," she fired back quickly.

"This place, money in the bank, the vineyard, the TV Company, the restaurant, my clothes, my car..."

"So it is just about money - even if you could die or get your brains mashed," she countered.

Suddenly he sat up and distanced himself from her.

"Do you think I don't know that?"

"I'm sure you do - that's why I ask."

"So - it's a risk - I calculate that risk," he sighed with an edge of exasperation.

"But this fight with Brennan - you don't need it," she said, wishing she could just open up and tell him everything of what she knew.

"Anna! You're sweet and loving but you know nothing of this vile business. I need this fight OK. One day I'll tell you all about the fight game - after it's over. If I start to mix philosophy with brutality I will end up on the floor," he replied with a cold finality.

Her heart lurched and she felt a stab of tears. She had spoiled things - something that was always going to be spoiled. She thought of the days ahead, towards the arrival of the mob lawyer Scapaticci in Nice. There was no possible need for Freddie to meet Brennan's manager! Their love should never have been, could never be - except that she loved him so deeply that she was nothing other than his.

"Freddie - I'm sorry," she sobbed, "I'm just so frightened of you being hurt."

"Oh baby," he said softening his voice and stroking her cheek, "I didn't mean to be harsh - I don't want some hard faced bitch who wants to talk about fights and wants me to beat some guy up so that I'm the champ. I love you as my soft baby who just knows me as a man…her guy who goes off and does some job somewhere. I'm champion because I've watched listened and learned, not because I'm a guy who wants violence."

"So how did you get started as a boxer?" she asked gently.

He smiled and lay back with his hands behind his head, "Look - if I get started on all that we'll be here all day - talking about myself to a soft beautiful girl with no clothes could really distract me," he joked.

"Just a quick sketch," she pleaded.

"I was born in France. My mother and father were students at the Sorbonne - just down the road. She was from a poor family who'd sacrificed a lot. She was studying international business. That's just a polite way of saying studying money! He was some kind of revolutionary poet, looking for the death of wealth, scribbling poems in pavement cafés. Somehow - somehow and don't ask me how - they fell for each other."

"So - it was ooh là là! - how romantic," she sighed.

"Exactly - romance but little else. She is pregnant, spurned by her family and married to this wild hippy guy who gets a job teaching literature in a little village with two cows, a boulangerie - and a school."

"For the cows?"

"In France, two cows mean fifty farmers and two hundred kids. I think there were some goats up one end of the village."

Anna laughed. His mood had changed and once again she burrowed blindly into her happiness.

"So - Mom winds up rolling cheeses and cooking rabbit, but dreaming of London, New York or at least Paris and a city job," he continued.

"And your father...?"

"He taught, began to establish himself as a top French poet, wrote philosophy - walked the fields with a notebook and a mongrel dog."

"Do you see him?" she asked, drawn to such a character.

"Yeah sure, but - well, he is not - um - proud of what I am and everything..." he faltered and stopped.

She sensed that there was far more to say but she decided not to push.

"So, one day Mathieu La Salle comes home to find the cottage empty and a sweet little note on the table explaining that his wife and little Freddie were flying to the USA."

"God - where did you go?"

"We touched down at LA and rented a room while she found work. Then we got a bus north to a trailer park in Castroville. It was all Mom could afford."

"Did you miss home - and your father?"

"Sure - I was a weird kid. We only spoke French in the house and at school. Mom spoke in English to me sometimes but I was struggling at first - I had a friend - a Mexican kid called Ramon. He only knew Spanish so I was like a genius. His folks were illegals and worked the artichoke fields. His big brothers were boxers and all dreamed of being Rocky and punching their way to wealth and fame. These guys looked after me and showed me how not to get bullied cos you're different."

"Poor baby - how old were you?" she asked tenderly, imagining him as a boy.

"I was about ten - Ramon was nearly eleven - he was really pleased that he was always gonna be older than me and that I could never catch him up…"

He stopped and his voice seemed to choke with emotion. She watched him sitting motionless and for a moment thought she saw tears in his eyes. She had learned that he was a complex man with walls inside him that only he would knock down.

He drew her to his chest and kissed the top of her hair.

"Your hair shines so beautifully," he said quietly.

She ran her hand down across the olive skin of his stomach and brushed his soft hair. His arousal was powerful and almost instant. Whatever had been his sadness, at least she could blot it out. She swung herself on top of him and slid him into her. This was Paris and they were nothing if they were not lovers.

When he had gone to shower she lay warm in his scent. His mobile lay on the Louis XVI table. She had time to check it out, find out who he knew and who called and when. She got up and wrapped herself in his gown. She would keep this until she died. How could she think of betraying him when his life force had surged into her longing belly just a few minutes before? She wandered out to the lounge and sank into the deep sofa. He appeared, wearing a pair of white briefs through which he bulged. His flawless skin glowed with health and strength. His face was newly shaved and impossibly handsome. He turned to her and smiled with his deep chestnut eyes.

"You don't look out of shape... the papers say you are not training," she commented as she took in his sculpted form.

"The papers don't always get it right - but believe me, once I go to California, it's work!"

"But this will be your last fight?" she asked nervously.

"Oh yes mon amour,"

"And will you be allowed a woman while you are training?" she half teased.

"There are no real rules - but for a week before the fight I'm on a different planet. It's about focus and aggression. You would not want to be there."

"And you will win?"

He looked at her seriously and nodded, "I will win,"

She did not want to push too far but suddenly thought of a tactic.

"Should I sell everything and put it on you to win? I could make a fortune," she asked disingenuously.

He looked at her stonily.

"Don't even dream of doing that."

"But, I believe you're going to win."

"I'll be the best man - but no one has muscles on their chin - it's boxing - some guy is trying to put your lights out. I am prepared and have the experience."

"Oh Freddie - I'm so afraid," she whispered.

"And that, ma belle, is why women do not come to training camp," he said finally, "let's look forward to a day in Paris."

She kissed him on the lips and slipped away to get herself ready. She chose her black culottes, pump shoes, a red satin blouse and the taupe linen blazer. As she emerged fragrant and elegant, he was on the phone. He mimed that it was Mom. Anna checked the time - it was 10.30am - That would be 4.30 a.m. in California.

"Mom - don't worry - I'll be with you Sunday - Sure I'll swing by the vineyard tomorrow and check out the figures with Christophe... no I haven't checked the dollar exchange rate yet."

He smiled across at her, rolling his eyes and shaking his head.

"Yah - I do have a girl - a very special girl - yah... she's perfect. Bye Mom... bye..."

He let out a sigh as he hung up.

"Sheesh - does she get up in the middle of the night to call you about business?" she questioned with a slight edge to her tone, filing away Mom's interest in his "girl".

"Why not Anna? She's fought her way up from nothing by looking after business," he stated in such a way that she realized that Mom was beyond reproach.

"Well, it is the middle of her night and she can't get in the ring with you," she replied, trying to convey that she was on his side.

"She doesn't need to - I guess you've never had nothing and had to stand up for yourself."

She swallowed an immediate response. It was not his fault if he did not know about her real life. She had gone into this with a deception in her heart. One day…one day he would know that she was not anyone's little girl! How he would react was a question still not asked.

"Freddie - I wasn't being personal or critical of her."

"I know that - but she lives for wealth and business - you were always Daddy's girl I guess. You didn't have to beat twenty guys to get your job."

Anna bit her tongue.

"Leyton Marine is a family business. Clients like to deal with family - so I out qualified everyone on this Earth," she responded hotly.

Freddie nodded and smiled, "I'll score that round to you baby," he said, obviously keen to defuse the situation.

He took her in his arms and kissed her. She felt a surge of love flow through her. One day she might ask his Mom if she was happy for her son to die or scramble his brains while she looked after business. Today was life enough and for today and she would live it.

Chapter 13

They walked hand in hand down le Boulevard St. Michel. They fell naturally into step. Now and then a passerby would do a double take and swivel to look at him. A few chic Parisiennes lost their cool and giggled behind a hand held to the lips. She caught the words, "Oui - c'est lui - Freddie."

He could have a hundred girls at his feet in as many minutes, but she felt no concern. The way he kissed her cheek now and then as they walked let her know that he was hers alone and she was his.

At Notre Dame they took the river bus and followed the Seine. Passing under le Pont Neuf he kissed so tenderly that she thought she would faint. Some tourists applauded and Freddie took their group photo with the Louvre as background.

"There are some paintings by Courbet in the Musée d'Orsay - maybe we can just call in and take a look," he suggested.

"You wrote a book on Courbet didn't you Freddie?"

"Ah - you have researched a little. Yes, it is called 'L'Origine Du Monde' after a painting by that name," he smiled with his sexy brown eyes.

For a while he spoke in French about Art and the guidance of his father. It was like a master class in painting. Never was she surer that such a man would not involve himself with criminals.

At the Musée he entered through a side door, avoiding the hordes of tourists. An official leapt up. It became clear that Freddie had given a large collection on indefinite loan.

"Will you ever want them back?" she asked, calculating their worth to be several millions of pounds.

"Hopefully not, if everything works out for me - beauty is for everyone to share Anna - except for you. Now you are only for my eyes," he said as he pulled her to him.

The gallery was beautiful - housed in an old railway station and crammed with some of the finest Art that the world had ever produced. In his presence she felt part of a sophisticated and intellectual society which was a million miles from the life of a cop - immersed in deviancy and squalor.

He looked at her, sensing a slight reflectiveness in her emotions.

"I catch a note of sadness in you sometimes Anna - something deeper than I would see in a girl who sold boats and just counted the beans," he said kindly.

His words slipped under her defenses. She wanted to spread herself out and talk with him - about what she knew of life - of its loneliness, its violence, passion and despair that she had come to measure as she had lived as a London detective. The paintings of exhausted dancers by Degas went beyond decoration and she could tell him, longed to tell him of the back rooms and sad scenes she had known behind the glamour of the city. Now his kind voice and his mind reaching out for her, threatened to release a well of un-cried tears.

"I was thinking it was sad that these guys often died in poverty, yet left us all this great art," she lied, hoping it would throw him off the trail.

"That is so - but I have seen sadness in you before - when we first met you were going back home to nothing and no one. At my restaurant you seemed sad when we were talking... "

Her mind flashed back to how she had felt a big stone in her heart at having to live through her lie with him. It was clear that he was on her case and had tuned to her mind and body so that he could feel her beyond her words.

"You pick up such tiny signals Freddie," she smiled sadly - half wishing that he would just press on now and open her. A few more words, a few more sweeps of the radar from his deep brown eyes and she was gone...

"What do you think boxing is mon amour? You know the guy is hurt because he dances away and tells you it didn't hurt. Truth is seldom reflected in a mirror. More often it is glimpsed through a prism or a keyhole. We are all detectives - watching for clues of one another."

Her heart pounded. Just what the hell did he know? She felt trapped in the beauty of the touch of their eyes. Finally she just said what was in her mind.

"I love you so much Freddie. I know it's not possible to feel this way but I do. I'm afraid I'll lose you somehow."

"I feel the same Anna - I'm not looking for Miss Perfect with shallow thoughts and glitzy fake smiles."

Something had happened the day they met and they had sailed off towards an unknown horizon. One day they would both know everything of each other and just maybe scramble off the ship with their love intact as it sank.

They took a light lunch in the magnificent gallery restaurant. She noted that he had made no calls and seemed unconcerned. Since she was undercover she decided to fire a torpedo. She was here on a job and colleagues expected feedback.

"I read on the net that the referee from your last fight ended up dead," she said nonchalantly.

Freddie smiled, "You English - you love your conspiracy theories. I suppose you read that the Mafia tried to fix the result and that the ref was supposed to give the win to the other guy when I got cut. I've read all that stuff - but no one had told me the script. I was beating him. I could tell he was up to something by trying to butt me at every chance. He was slow and I didn't let him get close. Then, he had taken a few punches as he tried to get inside and was exhausted. He just stopped - glanced over at his corner and launched his head into my face. It was crazy. The guy must have been nuts! It was like a football guy hiding the ball up his shirt and running the length of the field to score," Anna laughed at the image. He continued, laughing gently himself, "I thought the Mafia were those guys in gangster movies - You're the dirty brother who killed my rat stuff . I don't know any Italians who talk like Al Capone or make offers you can't refuse."

Anna's mind raced to the expected arrival of Scappaticci, the Mafia lawyer in Nice. He could be joking his way out of a corner. She reached across the table and took his hand, searching his eyes and feeling the horror of the cut over his brow.

"You won't get hurt like that again will you?" she said softly.

He shook his head in a tight lipped determination.

"No chance mon amour - just no way," he assured her.

She used a trip to the ladies room to send a quick text to Judy in London, "Leave Paris tomorrow - Freddie is innocent OK," she smiled to herself. He was her man and would always be.

When she returned to the table he was signing autographs for staff. When other customers realized he was so approachable, something of a queue formed. Strangers patted his back, a lady of about eighty kissed his lips, an American posed in a cowboy hat with both he and Freddie holding up fists. Anna imagined the photo being shown down an invisible path of unborn great grandchildren.

"Do you get tired of all the clamor?" she asked when everyone had gone.

"Yeah - like I get tired of the villa in Antigua, the champagne, my Nereus 74 motor boat when the saleswoman gets on with her job," he laughed. "It's all part of the business honey - and to be honest, I know how lucky I am."

"But you have had to fight!"

"Yes - so what? Life is a fight for some poor schmuck with no papers who breaks his back in the fields for a pittance - I've seen all that when I was a boy... "

His voice tailed off and he turned his attention to the traffic running past on the Quai D'Orsay.

She knew to stay quiet. She remembered how on a summer's day as a child the world suddenly grew still as a menacing hawk hovered over the English downland. She felt the same shadow now as he looked away with a tear visible in his eye. She too looked away at the other diners, giving him the space to recover. What was it that he could not express? What melancholy was it that reached out from his heart into hers? Was this the factor X that somehow they both knew and found in each other?

Within a few seconds he had moved on and took her hand, smiling.

"Let's take the river boat up to the Eiffel Tower and back to Notre Dame - I want to kiss you at every monument and under every bridge," he declared.

And he did. In the warm afternoon sun they stamped their own pattern of lovers onto the fabric of Paris.

Back at his penthouse he opened a bottle of Veuve La Salle and poured two glasses. She watched his assurance and self confidence. He got things right. It was warm enough to stand on the balcony as the evening started to deepen the clear sky. Here and there a light snapped on like an exclamation mark.

"Here's to us," he said seriously.

"And just what is 'us'," she echoed, slipping her arm around his waist and laying her head on his shoulder.

"I am asking myself this question every moment," he replied in his quirky French way of speaking English, "my life - maybe I can say - our lives are come to a crossroads - The poet Robert Frost, he has put it so well - we must take a path and leave another path not taken. Anna - you have trusted me - or maybe not trusted - rather you have thrown yourself from a plane hoping that your parachute will open."

"None of this would have been me Freddie - not my old self. I had a career, a plan - I knew where I was going... "

She pulled up, realizing that she had strayed and was about to start opening up the sealed envelope of her real life.

"You will take over Leyton Marine?" he asked quizzically, clearly surprised.

"Errr - modern management is more about marketing," she stumbled.

"And there is no one in your life - there must be boyfriends?"

"There is no one - there hasn't really been anyone," she answered. The last thing she wanted was to bring Beaumont Locke into the picture, "and anyway you must have a hundred girls."

He swallowed the compliment with a slight nod.

"Where there is celebrity and money, there are always girls."

"And gorgeous hunks who write books about artists and quote poetry," she added, giving his waist a squeeze.

"That peculiar guy is just for you Anna," he chuckled.

She thought seriously for a moment. She had been reckless in her affair with him.

"I have done what I have done out of love - just blind love Freddie - I know I should be playing hard to get - but if this time is all there is for us then I will have lived and I will regret nothing."

He swept her into his arms. She felt the softness of his lips on hers. She let herself sink into the deep brown of his eyes. She wanted to explain...

"I have not asked things that a girl should ask - I know that. I have not wanted to break the spell - there are considerations... you know, medical things if I can say it that way."

"I know, you trusted me and could have risked your life," he murmured.

"And so could you. We both have - out of love and passion - it has to be the only way to love like this."

"There has been no one - I am a clean machine," he smiled warmly at her, "there is the matter of babies - I suppose I just feel it is right with the right woman."

For a second she just floated on his words then brought herself down to reality.

"I know my body and its seasons. We are okay so far," she said with a gentle knowing kiss on his cheek.

"More than physical risk - I felt I was risking my heart. You have it Anna and I have never let it go before. I believe you will never let me down or betray me."

"Of course not," she gasped, "I couldn't do that," her heart churned. She felt sick to the core at her duplicity. She loved him. She loved him.

He drew a deep breath and held her waist as he looked into her deep gray blue eyes.

"There are things in my life - in my past - in my future that you do not know yet. I want you to understand everything but I know that you will not understand. You will just worry over nothing. Once this fight business is over we will have our whole lives," he explained, pleading for understanding in her eyes.

Now she had to think. If he was about to tell all - did she want to know? This gorgeous man was her lover and she had given herself up to him on instinct. Her career could go to hell! She felt a release as her decision freed her from all her conflicts as if a bowling ball had blasted away all the pins.

"Freddie - I love you and I trust you. Tell me everything, something or nothing and I will feel the same."

He smiled deeply at her.

"My father says that you always think that you are headed somewhere, that there is some bus stop ahead where you will know to get off and say - "Yes, this is the place," but there is no such stop - the view from the window and the other folk on that bus are your life and it is always now. Each minute is your stop and is your place."

"He is a philosopher," she replied.

"Yes - and he is poor with holes in his clothes and an old bike - and he is French - so don't try this at home kids," he joked.

The evening had closed in over Paris. Across the vista of the city, lights were fizzing against the dark like bubbles in a glass of champagne. He drew her inside.

"Time for a long soak in the bath - shall we save water and the planet?"

She had already seen the enormous roll top claw foot bath and the idea thrilled her.

"I'll do your back," she giggled.

When he went to run the water she chanced to check her mobile. A message had come in from London.

"Gino Scapaticci accompanied by known hit man Mauro Tondelli, arriving Nice on same flight. French police not advised since we are letting it run. Watch out - could get interesting! Call in when you can. Judy"

Back to the office she sighed inwardly.

He called her into the bathroom. He was already naked in the bath. She stripped and slithered in to face him, watching him soap his powerful pecs and shoulders.

"You are a god!" she murmured.

"I'll be Adonis - you can be Venus," he replied reaching out to cup her breast.

Chapter 14

They dined at the Meurice on the Rue de Rivoli. She had chosen her simple black knee length dress and high heels. Her raven hair shone and her lips deep red in an achingly beautiful contrast. She felt good about herself and thrilled to be in Paris on his arm. He had dressed in a dark gray casual suit with a crisp brilliant open necked white shirt that accentuated his bronzed complexion.

"Tomorrow we can drive down to Troyes. I need to check out some business at the vineyard," he said, matter of fact.

"Your Veuve La Salle is fantastic," she said, studying the strength of his jaw and his perfect white teeth as he spoke.

"It is not bad - maybe not the very best in France - but my sons will take it on and up. They will learn to know the soil."

"Sons?" she gasped. Was there something she didn't know?

"You look like the bearer of fine sons," he chuckled with a wicked appraising glance,"but I would like a little girl - one to break hearts like you."

Her own heart was pounding. She tried to speak but looked down in confusion. Her eyes swept back up to find his already fixed on her.

"Oh yes - there will be no one else but you. If not you then no one - if you wanted that," he said calmly, softening his eyes to match her own melting emotions.

"I think I have frightened you ma chérie."

The splendor and bustle of the restaurant faded away to nothing. The embroidered linen of the tablecloths, the exquisite foie gras, the rich deep Bordeaux wine in crystal glasses that caught the light from the Louis XVI chandeliers were all invisible. She saw nothing but him, his face and the love she felt reaching out to her from his eyes and holding her in a mesmerized trance.

"Freddie... you don't know me... you have to fight... everything could change after that."

"It will change and we will begin our lives together."

She was scrambling on loose rocks as a great landslip had started in her soul. She loved him but in front of that love stood her profession and his, guarding the treasure of love with merciless weapons.

"You could lose this fight and end up..." she began, unwilling to say what she thought - that he could be a blind dribbling patient for the rest of his life... or maybe worse or better... dead!

"Darling, let me be the judge of that... I am your man. Not your little boy."

"So what? Is a dead lover worth fewer tears than a dead son?" she asked with a harsh clarity.

He looked steadily into her face. She could tell that he now knew that she was a match for him and she wouldn't be bulldozed.

"You are a woman - these things are for men. It is not too modern I guess. I'll help with the dishes, I'll cradle the babies and I'll live as a man," he declared.

Anna watched his lips, wanting more than anything to kiss them. She knew the notion of pride, risk and honor just as much as he did. But she couldn't tell him! If only she could tell him the truth.

"Supposing it were me Freddie - risking my life, risking my health and brains - how would you feel?"

"I would, I would... I would stop you - lock you up in a palace," he joked trying to divert her.

"I'd call the cops.

"And some big guy in a uniform with a notebook would give me a medal and we'd have a beer together," he laughed.

Anna could not help but smile. Quite probably his assessment was spot on. She was about to counter with a hypothetical lady cop but some shred of shame prevented her. She was hammering at him when he had no chance to retaliate. Quite simply she could attack the truth of his life and he could only shadow box against her web of lies. Maybe he would have been content for her to scream a patrol car at 80 mph up the Brixton Road towards the report of a man running amok with a machete - but she would guess that he would not!

"I don't mean to nag," she said, watching his lips form into a smile.

"And if I battered Monsieur the boulder Brennan - it would still be violence and be just as bad," he said, watching her eyes for a response.

She took a deep breath and prepared her answer. She disliked inconsistency in argument but she would not hide this truth from him.

"I would sing if you killed him and he couldn't hurt you. You are my man and my lover. I know that it's appalling to say something so brutal and so selfish - but that's how I feel," she said with a hard sincerity and pitilessness that shocked her.

He grinned and took her hand, stroking the back with his thumb and raising her ring finger.

"So - ma belle Anna - it looks like I am making the right choice for my wife."

"Wife?" she repeated numbly, stupidly as if the word was foreign.

"Of course - with so many sons needed to run the vineyard and the other businesses," he said naturally with a Gallic shrug.

"Wife - if you want me then Yes! Yes - of course yes," she burbled as fireworks exploded, avalanches crashed down mountains, space rockets lifted off. She was on an Interpol mission. Mafia mobsters were gathering on the sidelines. She had already made love to a suspect and now she was going to marry him! If ever there was a moment to come clean it was now.

He was beaming, and then burying his face in his hands, repeating the words, "I can't believe it - I have found you from the whole world."

He pulled a Cartier ring box from his pocket, his powerful hand folded around it.

"Maybe it is a little you know - big. I'm sorry - but I am half American you know."

For a moment the box sat in the palm of his open hand. She watched his long dark lashes as his eyes studied it. Then he opened the box and at once the sparkle of the largest and most beautiful diamond reflected the light of the chandeliers in perfect rays as if he had opened a door from which the sound of a symphony filled the room. He slipped it on her finger.

"You are mine and I am yours," he said simply, as his eyes embraced hers in a ballet that swept her up and possessed her in its grip.

She blinked at the platinum band set with a 5 carat princess cut solitaire diamond.

"It fits... " she mumbled stupidly, ashamed that she could not rise above banal confusion.

"I stole - borrowed a ring from your flat to get the size... I was very bad."

"It is so so beautiful, beautiful, beautiful... "

"Not beautiful enough," he said.

"I can't find the words..." she began.

"The magic word was Yes - and you found it," he smiled.

She looked away. How could she go on? How could she deceive him? She was his woman. She was a detective, a fraud and a liar. He was her man and she loved him more than her own life. A battle raged in her mind and heart. She retreated onto safe ground.

"You decided to marry me at my flat after one taxi ride and one night?"

"Oh no - I am a boxer Anna, I cannot wait that long to react. It was raining and I was standing in the street...I saw the most beautiful girl I had ever seen and I knew... that if I did not act... then it would be too late."

She shook her head in wonder and disbelief. Could real life be like that? She looked at him - and knew that it was like that. Just like that!

"I must tell someone," she said, bursting with joy, despair and the loneliness of her false life.

"Maybe your mother. You never seem to be in touch - but I guess you talk to them all the time about the business."

It would have been the natural thing to do, but she had hardly spoken to her since she had rejected the family firm and had moved to London as a cop. Her mother had planned a life for her and it did not involve crime and violence. As she thought she realized that her time with Beaumont had reduced her own circle of friends down to zero. Judy was her closest confidante and it was by no means certain that she would approve.

"I'll let it wait - I'll just wrap myself up in you," she said, focusing on the beautiful ring.

That night they made love tenderly, without urgency or complication, reaching out to each other like the roots of two seeds blown by chance and woven together as one. At around midnight they lay together in the moonlight. The window was a little open and admitted sounds from the street. In the distance voices and traffic spoke the muffled language of other lives. Somewhere close by in another apartment a sad saxophone played reflective moody late night jazz. If there had ever been a moment when she would have stopped time it would have been then - in the mellow moments of their after-love and their before-life. The great River Seine rippled and pushed on to the sea as the sun tip-toed the back stairs of the world climbing towards dawn across Paris. Maybe the morning light would never uncover two lovers hiding within the protection of each other's arms...

Chapter 15

The following morning they drove to Troyes. She could not resist looking at the ring every few minutes - convincing herself that it was real - that any of this was real. By lunchtime the Mercedes slipped into the courtyard of Freddie's champagne vineyard. He led her into the kitchen of a magnificent stone walled farmhouse. The smell of savory food, the cooking range, the flag-stoned floor, the enormous wooden table laden with cheese, poultry and wine brought an involuntary "Wow" from her lips.

Freddie introduced her as his fiancé to a procession of staff. She smiled and chatted in French, exhibiting the ring, holding up her hand and wriggling on an invisible glove. He took the time to warn them that Mom had not been told and that they were the first to know.

"Monsieur - you are so very brave!" exclaimed a rosy cheeked woman, embracing Anna.

"Not a word... if she calls just tell her I was with a fairy tale princess."

Evidently the vineyard workers had a good idea that Mom might not wish to come second in anything.

They ate a light non alcoholic lunch, whilst the staff freely celebrated the great event with jugs of wine, several bottles of champagne and all manner of meat and cheese. An old man of about eighty hugged Freddie around the neck, then bounced on his feet and jabbed out as if he were a boxer. Freddie's face beamed as he took a stance and sparred lightly with his elderly opponent. As he moved she almost gasped at his physical grace. His body was fluid and quick like a spring. He moved like a deer with speed and delicacy. He was truly beautiful. Finally he raised the old guy's arm as the victor and poured him a huge glass of champagne, and let him melt away into the crowd.

"That man was middleweight amateur champion of France before the war," he told her passionately, "he comes to work every day - I am so proud to know him."

"Does he work here?" she asked, wondering what he could do.

"He kinda checks stuff out,"

"Do you pay him?"

"Ummm - yeah," he replied thoughtfully, "Madame is thinking of the purse strings... this is good - but you know life is not fair - sometimes we have the luck to be alive and able to change things a little," he said with a firmness that she realized was a hint of a deep side to his nature. She kissed his cheek and let her kiss translate itself into words - through the dictionary of their love.

When Freddie went to the office with the vineyard manager, she took the chance to walk outside. She called the office.

"Yo! How's the big city?"

"Anna - God, I've been worrying - are you OK?" asked Judy urgently.

"Sure - why wouldn't I be OK?"

"Nothing - nothing specific - this guy Tondelli is a real killer - he's gonna be with the lawyer who manages Brennan. Beaumont thinks you ought to be pulled out - he wants to know if you call in. Christine Jones has told him to back off and let it run."

"She's right - I'm fine - these guys don't even land in France until tomorrow - anyway there's something else - something far more important," Anna hesitated, unsure of how to break such momentous news.

"What... what?" squealed Judy excitedly, picking up on Anna's manner.

She took a deep breath. She was on the edge of a platform, looking over into a canyon. Once she said a word it was free fall with no way back. Her palms sweated.

"I'm going to marry him," she declared abruptly.

There was a silence as she plunged downwards.

"Judy...?"

"What? What? Have you told him... does he know?" she shrieked. Anna laughed nervously at her friend's odd humor.

"Of course he knows - he's given me the most beautiful Cartier diamond ring... I wish you could see it."

"Do you know what the hell you are doing?"

She thought for a second - it was a sound question.

"Sure - we're gonna have sons to run the champagne business - oh - and a girl for him to spoil."

"What? Bloody hell, I mean God - I mean it's wonderful - you're nuts!"

"I'm nuts and it's ecstasy," replied Anna dreamily, "he's in the clear - I just know."

"So why is he meeting these mobsters?"

"Well, I'll find that out won't I," she stammered, unable to fire back a reflex answer, "anyway he hasn't said he's meeting anyone."

"Ok Anna - I know you're cool with this - I won't mention to the Commander that you are going to marry the suspect and have his babies. It may just be too much for the morning conference to swallow. We need everything off his phone. You've got the blank SIM card so go girl! We have got to show contacts to back up evidence of conspiracy... geddit?"

Anna nodded and smiled. Judy was right to bring her down to focus. She had a job to do.

"I feel so bad going behind his back when he loves and trusts me," she sighed, almost sick with the thought of it.

"Then don't get caught honey! And keep your eye on the ball - I'm worried about you," ordered Judy, completely oblivious to the superior rank of her friend.

She felt a slight stab of resentment. No one knew him like she did! This was the sort of idea that she had wanted to escape from when she had not admitted to being a cop.

"It's not just a case of being caught - it's a case of what I can take emotionally - I love him."

"Oh - honey - I can see that - look, just work to show he is innocent. Freddie is not the target here."

She heard his voice inside the farmhouse and ended the call. Luckily Judy was not compromised by the same passions. Here she was - standing in the back yard of a fabulous building with ducks and geese around her feet. Vines stretched away into the distance over the soil that could be the nursery of her children. Her man - her bull, poet and lover was about to appear. Between her and the dream stood a lie that robbed her of her future. She had to go on. She would have to copy the files from his phone and soon everything that she could see in front of her would be ripped away and trodden in the mud of mistrust and deception. The woman he loved was an Interpol detective who was there to spy on him.

What was it that his father had said - that our lives are not the bus stop ahead but the bus itself and the view from the window. So - she would live each second with no thought for the next - if she could.

She wandered back to the house, getting a grip of her raging emotions.

"Chérie - I'm sorry. I had to deal with a little business," he said openly, placing a gentle kiss on her lips.

His caring manner doubled her shame. Thoughts tumbled like random items from a sack. Time and time again she asked herself what it was that he would not discuss when he clammed up. Time and time again she asked why he had agreed to this fight and why, oh why oh why were two gangsters associated with the fight flying in to Nice - one of them his opponent's business manager and the other a killer?

She loved him. She loved him.

"I love you," she said almost desperately.

"Hey - chérie - what's up? Some little cloud has come across your sunshine," he said gently.

"Sometimes I worry that you don't know me - this is all so beautiful - maybe I don't deserve all this. Maybe I'm not what you need or what you think I am," she said, tearfully, searching his face for understanding and compassion.

"Ah - yes the old wooden leg trick - it's OK - the moment I fell in love with you I knew you had a wooden leg," he teased.

"I haven't got a wooden leg," she laughed, in spite of her feelings.

"Then it is all over - I only wanted a woman with a wooden leg - but I was too shy to tell you," he responded, reaching down and squeezing her thigh.

The way he dismissed her words only increased his vulnerability. He had a way of joking his way out of corners - almost desperate not to wake up from this dream. She tried again.

"I'm trying to be honest - I'm just so afraid I will disappoint you."

His mood calmed and he became serious, "Anna, listen - whatever there has been, whatever worries you - it is nothing. Nothing. We have both lived lives. There will have been highs and lows. I am not a fool. The day before we met was the last day of history. Since I saw you there has been only present and future. I love you as you are this moment. I love you for whatever has brought you to me. Love resets all the pieces on the chessboard."

He took her in his arms and kissed away all her resistance and all her resolve. Within herself she settled back into a comfortable seat to watch her own story unfold, took her hands from the steering wheel and headed breakneck towards the next curve.

"We can drive on to Lyon. I have fixed an hotel," he said.

"Lyon - why Lyon?" she questioned, her heart leaping with the knowledge that Lyon was home to the headquarters of Interpol and there would be a very increased risk of being recognized."

"It is half way to Antibes and I want to show you the old town and the Basilica. I am interested in the marble and the mosaics. One day I would like to study the art of churches - I guess you have never been there," he replied with boyish enthusiasm.

"No - no, never," she lied, immediately aware that her impulse to lie had probably made things worse. If she was spotted, it would have been easier to explain if she had been there!

The Mercedes swallowed an afternoon ribbon of road.

"I must call my father tonight," she said, aware that his meeting with Freddie was closing in and that it was far from certain that he would help with the deception that she was weaving.

"Call now - from the car," he suggested.

"Oh - it'll be a long call - no need to put it on the cell phone - I'll call from the hotel."

He smiled and shook his head.

"Madame will be a great guardian of my wallet. Anyone would think that you were a poor little ant scraping along to pay your bills."

If only he knew. How she dreaded talking to her father. There was no reason why he would want to compromise his business by acting as a front for the police. There was potential for huge damage to the Leyton Marine brand.

"How does it feel when you step in the ring?" she asked innocently enough - wanting to know more of him.

"Focused I suppose. You hear the crowd but you are not aware of what they are shouting."

"Do you feel fear?"

"Of course - afraid of being on your back with everything gone. You are only ever one punch away from defeat - but now I feel very different."

"How?"

"Because there is someone in my life who wants me win or lose -

not some trash who wants only the champion - there are plenty of those."

"This will be the last fight won't it - promise me Freddie," she begged - her heart breaking at what he had said. How had she got into this position? He trusted and respected her. She loved him desperately. Soon everything would be spoiled like virgin snow turned to slush. He would fight in a rigged match while strangers shrieked and rejoiced in his blood. Criminals would gloat on their winnings and she could not be there at his side. She began to sob uncontrollably.

"Baby - please...it'll be a tough fight, but I can handle it. I trust you and I'm asking you to trust me. I can't bear to see you so sad," he replied reaching across for her hand.

His touch and his words made her despise herself even more. She had spent ten years listening to the lies and fabrications of criminals and had come to loath dishonesty. Now she had become no better.

"I'm OK - I'm sorry, I trust you my dear sweet man. You'll win and it will all be fine."

"I won the day we met Anna," he said with a solid authenticity that almost stopped her heart - like a knockout - like a last word.

She leaned back into the leather as the big smooth car ate the distance. It was dusk when they arrived at the hotel Florentine in the old town quarter of Lyon. Anna had also come to love the place during her visits. A smell of wood smoke haunted the narrow cobbled streets while the illuminated Basilica looked out across the Roman tiled Gallo-Romano rooftops. She wanted to phone her father in private but Freddie had become playful. She hung up a few items of clothing, feeling the stroke of his eyes probing her body. She watched him carelessly undress and lie down naked, not speaking but transmitting waves of man power. From the corner of her eye she caught sight of his arousal. Despite all the turmoil in her mind she felt herself responding. He intercepted her thoughts.

"I'm sorry chérie - it's not my fault that you turn me on so much - I can't help it - I need therapy," he said in a mock pleading voice.

She smiled, feeling a dull awakening in her belly and the tension in her nipples. Her eyes dilated and hot desire swept over her. She abandoned all her worries and let them fall crumpled with her knickers and discarded shoes as she walked to him, gazing into his eyes with her deep dark pupils wide open and her hands releasing her belt. She straddled him and pushed him flat onto the bed. He groaned and drew her breast into his mouth. She plunged her wet longing down onto his silky steel erection. He filled and caressed her as she moved rhythmically in slow pulses above him. She caught his male musk of his skin and thought of his sperm bursting into her female flesh - deep deep into her craving core. She pressed her lips down onto his. His tongue met hers, teasing away the last shred of reserve. She shuddered and looked down at his closed eyes lost in a dream of ecstasy.

Behind the lids of his eyes he sensed her moment. Now he was driven on by her sweet gripping succulence. He tensed his buttocks to drive himself into her, letting himself go in thrusts of wordless animal pleasure.

She subsided onto his chest as he kissed her neck in time with his echoing shocks of release. She wanted to draw him in and squeeze every juice from the sweet fruit of lust.

"You are woman," he groaned, "utter joy of woman my angel."

His words mixed with his male scent. She let her soft breasts press onto his rippled body. She floated in a timeless heaven - before the complications of words - in the jungle of shameless desire and the steaming swamps of passion.

She ran her hand across his scarred brow and kissed his lips.

"I love you," she said simply.

"And I you... more than I can put into words," he murmured dreamily.

Somewhere in the room his mobile was ringing. He scrambled in his discarded clothing to find it.

"Hi Mom - yeah - I'm fine. What? What guy? Um - Scapaticci - Have I met him before?"

Anna came to attention. This was business. The call continued.

"He wants to talk about a project you say - what's that - he'll open with an investment of ten million dollars - are you sure?"

Anna watched his face. He seemed relaxed and unaware who this guy was.

"OK Mom - I'll wait for his call - sure I'll be nice OK - I mean that's a lot of money..."

She lay still on the bed trying to appear uninterested, as he finished the call.

"You sound like a hire and fire tycoon," she commented, trying to sound a bit naïve and girly.

He grinned, "Some lawyer guy wants to meet me tomorrow at his hotel in Antibes - he's got some way of making money. There's zillions of ideas out there honey - I meet these kinda guys all the time."

Anna smiled back. What was the project? What did Mom know - could she fail to know that Scappaticci was Brennan's business manager? She decided to push a little.

"Ten million dollars is a lot of money."

"Yeah - in some ways," he replied.

His vague answer irritated her and for a second she felt of stab of anger. He wanted to marry her but locked her out of his affairs. Before she could rein in her response she had fired a question as if she were interviewing a suspect.

"No one gives away ten million dollars without some tough pay back conditions surely?"

He looked up at her calmly but with steel in his eyes.

"Anna - you cannot know the boxing business and I'm not gonna start explaining it to you. I want you outside the ring. My career is nearly over and that's all you need to care about. One day I'll fill you in but for now I love you as you are and that is enough. I never want to argue with you about this baby - but this is my world - and I run it."

She sat heavily on the bed, feeling his words as if they were punches. She let her head drop down and didn't look at him.

"You know that there were crooks involved in your last fight - I'm worried that's all."

"But you don't know anything - I don't know anything. It's all guesses and Sherlock Holmes stuff - you know all that deduction that it was a left - handed bald man with limping dog."

She looked up and smiled at him with tearful eyes.

"The dog didn't limp," she said.

He softened his eyes and put his arm around her.

"Baby - it'll all be fine. Let the detectives worry about the crooks. You're my sweet lover, that's all I need. You will learn everything - when I write the book."

"But why do they target you?" she persisted.

"Who says anyone is targeting me? You must know more than I do! This Scappaticci is just a business guy and he's got in touch with Mom. Perhaps he just wants me to market some trainers or perhaps he's dreamed up some dumb gum sweet and wants me to chew it for the cameras."

"For ten million dollars?" she fired back.

"Yeah - it is a bit cheap," he laughed,"hey, come along to the meet and tell him we want twenty. Call your pa - I'll take three of those boats!"

Anna could not help but smile. Whenever she began to corner him he could joke his way out. She kissed his cheek. She knew he could sense her unease and tension - although, poor guy, he thought it was entirely his fault and could not guess at the truth.

"This life - there are... there are sorrows - things we try to live through, things that are always on your mind. Trust me - just love me and trust me. You won't get this - but your love will see me through," he said, suddenly hugging her as if for comfort.

She knew not to push him now. This was real. She had reached that barrier inside him that sometimes hinted but melted like a wounded deer into the forest. She held him, feeling his need for her tenderness and love like never before. He was champion of the world and for the first time through their shared rhythms, she experienced his loneliness almost as if it had been her own.

"I'm gonna shower," he announced suddenly, breaking away, not turning his face to her, "the restaurant here has a Michelin star like my place in London - I want to check the standard - and maybe the chef," he called from the bathroom.

She sat still on the bed, reaching her hand up to her shoulder where he had laid his head. She drew her hand back to her lips and tasted the salt of a tear.

Chapter 16

She dialed her father's number on the hotel phone. She imagined the house in Sandbanks overlooking Poole harbor. The neighbors were a North London football team manager and a gray frail punk rocker from the 70s who wore a peaked hat and walked a poodle. It was a long way from her flat in Kilburn.

"Dad!"

"Anna!"

She had not thought through what to say - she could hardly tell him that in five days she had become engaged to the client.

"I'll be at Antibes tomorrow afternoon," she began, "we're in Lyon - um - things changed a bit."

"Lyon? Are you planning to show him around the Interpol headquarters?" he asked with an edge of sarcasm.

"Dad - it's fine - I'll explain everything - just trust me."

"I'm worried Anna. If clients think that Leyton Marine is a police front it will really hurt us."

She sighed. He was right. He was so right and she was selfishly using anything to get what she wanted. Except that she had lost sight of what she wanted.

"I'll make sure it's OK Dad - I promise - I love you."

"I love you too Baby. I've got a meeting in La Rochelle. I'll fly the chopper down after lunch."

She rang off as Freddie walked in with just a small towel around his waist.

"Did you tell him his little angel is running off with some prize fighter?" he smiled, sitting beside her and kissing her neck. She quivered as if a jolt of electricity had shot through her.

"I'll tell him when we're face to face. You haven't told your mother," she said, trying to distract him. If her father didn't know, then it was all still a dream and she would be able to wake up without all the consequences. Her father would tell her mother and then the hounds would come yelping out of hell to chase her down. Her beautiful princess, who had run off to live in the gutter, was now to marry a brawling gorilla!

"The Nereus is a beautiful boat," she said as if to concentrate on business.

"Sure - at that price it's got to be good," he replied with a rueful grin, "I've got salt in my blood. When Mom moved to Monterey I had a fishing boat and used to go out catching dinner and seeing all those fantastic whales and stuff."

"Fishing? The Nereus is not a fishing boat."

"I know - it was a thing left over from being kids - you know Ramon - the kid from the trailer park- he dreamed of having a boat - wanted to catch food for the family. We used to fish off the beach or off the pier at Santa Cruz," he stopped and seemed to be thinking.

"Where have you gone Freddie?" she asked, tossing a pebble into his lake of contemplation. He did not respond. She knew this was not a spot to push, that just beneath the skin was a bruise. She watched him looking down like a boy who had scuffed his new shoes playing football.

She kissed his cheek and sprang up. It was time to get ready for dinner. She glanced back at him, still sitting on the bed. There was something in his soul that made him both unknowable and more loveable. He was world cruiser-weight champion - one of the toughest guys on the planet - and yet there seemed to be no trace of violence within him. Only when she pushed at his office door did she see the iron in his soul. That world of meetings with Mafia lawyers and what he had called "the project" was off limits. As a cop she knew it looked bad. Maybe for the final time she bundled up all the debris of her fears and desires and stored them out of sight. She showered, brushed her raven hair until it shone and dressed in her beaded oyster top and matching trousers. She added a little perfume, took a deep breath and thought of food.

"You're incredibly beautiful," he whispered as they entered the restaurant.

He looked doubly gorgeous in a beige jacket, white silk shirt and black trousers. The width of his shoulders seemed to expand each time she looked at him.

The Maitre D' only too aware of who Freddie was, showed them to a secluded table by a window overlooking the city. As they sipped aperitifs her heart began to leap and thump inside her chest so that she was breathless. Entering the restaurant was Inspecteur Raymond Du Maurier of Interpol - the very man who had sent her Freddie's file. He spotted her immediately and excused himself from a group of Chinese men. Anna immediately realized that they were a visiting delegation of Hong Kong police officers - one of whom she had met at a conference.

"Anna!" he gushed as he approached the table at full speed.

She decided she had to go for broke...

"Ciao - Signor Pandolfi . Che grande sorpresa - come va?"

Inspecteur Du Maurier stopped with a quizzical expression on his face, searching Anna's eyes for clues as to what was going on.

"Ah - si," he began, mercifully picking up on her urgent signals.

"Ti prego - dire nulla," she urged.

She could see that he was thinking. From somewhere she had recalled that Du Maurier had worked with the Italian art squads and that he spoke Italian. She was fairly sure that Freddie did not.

"Capito," he replied - glancing at Freddie and catching on that something very unusual was unfolding. She had to be careful. Her lover had lived in California and had a good grasp of Spanish and could easily pick up on Italian. She hit him with an animated tidal wave of Italian on the subject of a fictitious motor cruiser moored at Rimini that Signor Pandolfi had purchased from Leyton Marine.

Then she introduced him to Freddie, who stood, smiling.

"Grand plaisir," said the Inspecteur falteringly as if these were his only words of French.

The Chinese guys shuffled awkwardly as a waiter battered them in incomprehensible French. Du Maurier backed away to rescue his guests, speaking back to the waiter in Italian as they were shown to a distant table.

Freddie was delighted.

"God - you are so fantastic Anna - speaking in Italian - God I love you more and more."

Anna sat down gratefully and tried to look urbane and cool while her heart still pounded.

"What a strange little guy," he chuckled, "why is an Italian wandering around in France with a gang of Chinese guys?"

"He has an auto components business with a big office here in Lyon. They supply Renault and have a lot of the parts made in China. I just know him because he bought a boat a couple of years back," she answered casually.

Freddie nodded seriously as he accepted the tale. The breadth and depth of her dishonesty appalled her. She had become an instant fantasist. She drew the story from an Interpol case involving fake car brakes. The boat in Rimini was pure off the cuff dreamland. One day he would realize that his lover was a liar. Maybe he would never know the extent of her undercover training - she could hardly tell him now!

After dinner they took a stroll in the old town. The air was cool and slightly damp forming melancholy haloes around the dim street lamps. She snuggled into him as he swept his muscular arm around her. She felt a profound sense of safety and protection in his grip. Their love was rolling on beyond mad attraction. She knew that ahead must be a crash. He talked of his plans for sons, for the vineyard, for a restaurant in Paris. He dreamed of summer days at sea, picnics with champagne, a house in San Francisco. She listened, knowing that she would never be part of his future. It would be a case of what she could salvage from the wreck of her life that could be minutes, hours or days away.

That night, they did not make love but lay spooned like puppies in a litter. For the first time in her life she knew the profound passion of sleep within the soul of another being.

Chapter 17

It was 7.30 am when she saw the face of her mobile light up. The office would only contact an undercover officer in emergency. Freddie lay sleeping. She squinted at the screen. The message was direct from Judy:

"Scappaticci and Tondelli both at hotel in Juan-Les-Pins, Beaumont going nuts and wants you pulled out. Christine Jones has overruled him and says she just wants results. We need to know what is on his phone! I'm up early because Raymond Du Maurier phoned me at home to check things out. Told me you were nearly uncovered and that photos of you with Freddie in Paris are all over the French gossip magazines. Money still pouring on Brennan. Keep safe and stay in touch."

Anna lay back thinking. She had a job to do. They needed to show conspiracy between the players. Good or bad she loved him and would be there for him. The truth was the truth and it had to be known.

She saw his mobile on the table beside the bed. She slipped out and recovered the blank SIM card that Judy had hidden in her laptop case. She grasped his mobile and crept to the bathroom and sat on the toilet. The phone was switched on. It was a familiar model that she knew how to handle. In seconds she had the removed the battery and SIM card and punched in a default code. Ninety seconds later the contents of his phone were stored on the card. She replaced his old card and switched on. It was pin protected. She used the bidet, dried and slid back into the room as he began to stir. She tossed the phone on the floor by his bed, and then entered from his side, kissing his lips as she straddled him with her legs. Her awakened soft groove pressed invitingly on his chest. He looked up knowingly and pulled her hips forward, caressing her with his tongue.

"I think I knocked your phone on the floor," she gasped as the first delicious tremors of pleasure began to tremble through her.

A while later as Freddie dressed she slipped the pirated card into a hotel envelope. When he had picked up his phone he had merely commented that the jolt had switched it off and re-entered his pin. His innocence and trust hurt her to the core. She had crossed a bridge and there was no way back.

"I've given the hotel number to the office. I'm half expecting a fax about some fabrics for next year's models," she lied as they sat at breakfast.

He nodded and smiled unconcernedly as she walked to the reception desk and handed over the envelope.

"A Monsieur Du Maurier will call for this envelope later today. Can you see he gets it?"

"Oui Madame."

"Merci."

"Je vous en prie."

And to betray her lover, her man and her future - it was as easy as that.

With a trip to the bathroom she sent a text to Judy, "SIM card in envelope at reception - Hotel Florentine, Lyon. Ask Raymond to collect."

Chapter 18

As the Mercedes sped south on the autoroute, she relaxed into a state of shame. At least by being professional she knew what she was. By the time they reached their destination, Interpol would know everyone that Freddie knew. She watched his handsome tanned face. Over and over she asked herself how she could ever lie to him or hurt him. And the answer came. It was the same answer she gave to herself when they had met in London and she had opened their affair with a lie. She was a cop.

They cruised into Antibes in the mid afternoon. He drove with the window down, catching the scent of the sea and the slight trace of excitement on the southerly wind that swept in a hint of Africa.

They parked on the Millionaire's Quay and walked hand in hand along the pontoon. The Nereus 74 languished alongside, pure white and deep blue, with an air of sharpened predatory menace. It had been designed by Mike Leyton and formed the corner stone of his billion dollar business.

They were greeted at the vessel by the uniformed resident crew, Bertrand and Lucienne, a husband and wife team. Anna, who had known them most of her life, hugged and kissed them, introducing Freddie - although clearly they knew exactly who he was.

"You are so brave alone on the streets of London," said Lucienne, "your father tells us about the dangers..."

"Oh - he believes what it says in the papers, she interrupted hastily, realizing that they would know nothing of her deception.

"Are you guys really gonna let me take your baby out to sea tomorrow?" asked Freddie, beaming at the prospect, "I've got my United States Coast Guard Masters Certificate."

"Certainement - Anna knows these waters," replied Bertrand.

After a tour of the boat, Freddie positioned himself in the driving seat. He looked awesome in his T shirt and faded Dolce and Gabbana jeans. His broad neck and shoulders stretched the cotton fabric across the rounded curves of his muscles. His large strong hands touched the controls. It was obvious that he knew his way around power craft. She left him chatting with Bertrand excitedly about all the boy's toys on the bridge and went below decks with Lucienne.

"Anna - I have known you so many years - I couldn't help but notice that you were hand in hand on the pontoon..."

As the older woman spoke, her eyes caught the glint of the Cartier diamond on Anna's finger.

"Alors - Mon Dieu - you are engaged! I am so happy - he is so wonderful, so everything," she exclaimed.

Anna smiled weakly, "Lucienne - if only things were that simple. Yes, we're engaged - I love him - he wants me but..." she stopped as tears forced their way past her strength and resolve. Being with someone warm who knew her suddenly released all the tension of the past few days, "it's all a sham. It can never be. It could all have been so different."

"It can't be so bad - if there is love then there is love. I can see it in his face."

Anna sank down into the sumptuous white leather sofa, sobbing with her face buried in her hands.

"It is a long story - I didn't tell him I was a cop."

Lucienne let out a breath, "So what - you are you and that's it...we could tell him now and I know he wouldn't care."

"Anna - where are you? You are not doing much of a sales job," called Freddie from above.

"I'm just preparing for your inspection Captain," she replied, dredging up pretense - yet another deception. How sick she was of the whole slithering pile of lies.

She dried her eyes and took a deep breath before climbing back to the top deck. The afternoon sun was warm on her skin as her eyes adjusted to the light catching on the water. Around the harbor, billions of dollars worth of motor cruisers and yachts gleamed idly on their moorings. The sea was calm and varied from aquamarine through to turquoise beneath a clear blue sky above an horizon dotted with salt-swept cypress. These few days should have been the happiest of her life, but from one small lie her dream had transformed into a hideous nightmare.

Freddie was like an excited kid, pointing out the satellite navigation system and the radar sweep on a screen.

"I can't wait to push these babies forward," he declared playfully, placing one hand on the throttles and the other on Anna's butt.

She squealed, secretly glad that his mind was distracted from her tearful countenance.

His mobile started to ring. He sighed and pulled it from his jeans.

"Uh - yeah - sure Scappaticci - yeah, I know about it - Juan-Les-Pins OK - about an hour I guess."

He hung up and looked at her with a roll of his eyes, "A bit of business honey. Hotel Juana - d'ya know it?"

"Gorgeous Art Deco - you'll love it," she replied, her heart sinking. So it was real. He was about to meet a Mafia front man who doubled as Brennan's manager. Should she tell him to watch out for Tondelli? Should she tell him now and tell him exactly how she knew?

He eased himself out of the seat, patting Bertrand heartily on the shoulder.

"Merci - Capitano. Tomorrow we will see what she can do."

"If you can handle this you'll be able to handle Billy Brennan," commented the uniformed skipper.

"That man is nothing - these women worry you know," he replied with a wink at Lucienne who almost blushed, "this fight will be interesting. I used to worry about saving my looks for the ladies.

Now I have the girl of my dreams - perhaps I can put on a show and risk my beautiful nose. Read the papers and they tell you I am out of shape. Let's see at the weigh in. Bertrand - remember everything I've told you."

Anna relaxed a little. Evidently he had been talking to Bertrand in some kind of exchange of male bonding. Soon enough he would be stepping into a boxing ring to face a brutal conclusion to his career. His words fascinated her. She was no expert but he did not look out of shape! He was pure muscle without an ounce of fat.

He threw an arm around her as they walked to his car.

"It was great to hear you talking about the fight - what did you tell him?" she asked softly.

"You would only worry ma belle. That guy knows the business a little - we chatted about jabs and hooks."

She decided to let it ride. Just beneath the surface her emotions threatened to overwhelm her. They drove to the heli-pad at Port Vauban where she kissed him on the lips and waited for her father. She watched the Mercedes pull away. A small white car seemed to move off at the same time, driven by a male in a dark suit. Anna noted the coincidence and the odd clothing of the driver. He was slightly out of place - always the first whisper in the ear of a cop. Out of habit she memorized the vehicle number. In the distance she heard the beat of a helicopter rotor. Now this would be a challenge - as if she needed one!

Chapter 19

The new Augusta Grand VIP chopper resplendent in its Leyton marine livery sank down onto the pad. The turbines whined down as Mike Leyton pulled off his headphones and stepped out into the lengthening shadows of the afternoon.

She threw herself into his arms as he straightened up, clear of the rotors.

"My baby. My baby," he said reassuringly in his deep voice.

"It's so good to see you Dad. So much has happened."

"Let's take a stroll back to the boat and analyze the situation," he said calmly.

In his presence she felt relieved, as if her burden were halved. His white hair flowed back. His ruddy face was strong and exuded competence. She poured out her story.

"I didn't know who he was - we shared a cab - I wanted to get away from being a cop - just be a woman like any other - I told him I sold boats because I know this business - then I get myself assigned to his case and he wants to marry me and I love him. It's so simple really!"

Mike Leyton shook his head, lifting her hand to look at the ring as if to convince himself that something was real.

"So - you spend ten years as a street cop and detective dealing with every known depravity of mankind. Then one day you meet an unknown guy in the street, fall in love and just go with the flow as if you were a new born babe."

She reflected on his summary of events, smiling at the apparent absurdity of her story.

"I think that sums it up pretty well. He wants sons, a girl to spoil and to live at his champagne vineyard," she added with deliberate understatement.

"If he escapes Interpol, the Mafia and twelve rounds in the ring..."

"Yes..."

"That Beaumont was such a pompous fraud," declared Mike, changing the subject with a laugh, "If you had told me you were going to marry him it would be serious."

Anna felt a flood of warmth as he hugged her, he was on her side. Somehow things would work out.

They arrived at the boat and went down to the saloon. Chocolate brown deep pile carpet set off the white Moroccan leather suite. He went to the walnut cocktail cabinet and mixed two large vodka martinis and joined her on the sofa.

"What happens - do you have a secret transmitter hidden in your bra?" he questioned with a wicked twinkle in his blue eyes.

"I took his phone and copied the files," she answered ashamedly.

"He need never know that Anna - never never. For as long as you live never tell him."

"Should I not be fully honest one day?"

"No - he loves you and perhaps he could cope with you going along with the job because you wanted to be near him. One day he will see that you were prepared to put yourself in danger for that reason. If he learned you went behind his back he would never trust you."

She nodded, conceding the point. He need never know.

Her father took a slug of his drink, "Where is your future husband anyway?"

"He's meeting a Mafia guy who manages Brennan," she replied flatly.

"What? Are you going to lock him up and marry him in jail?"

"It's a bit of a mess Dad," she said lamely as tears began to roll down her cheeks.

"The fact is that he probably is involved Anna. Why get beaten up when he can just get a big pay day and walk off as a multi millionaire."

"I can see all that. I wouldn't blame him and I would love him anyway."

"Then you have to put your cards on the table. You can't run with the hare and hunt with the hound," he insisted.

"You're right..."

"For myself I don't want swaggering mobsters fixing up sport for their own greed. To a lot of ordinary folk these heroes are everything. And I do not want my business used as an undercover police front. Such a story could ruin us!"

"I know, I know. I've been so selfish - so stupid, so blind."

"That's about as good a description of true love as I've ever heard," he half chuckled, "the solution is going to start with telling him the truth."

"Can it wait until after the sea trial? He is so excited - like a kid with a train set."

Mike Leyton thought seriously, "Let's hope he doesn't find out from the mobsters - I guess you'll know soon enough. It's got to be your call. Let's all meet up for dinner at La Marmite at 8.30. I'm going to take the chance to fly down to Monaco - looks like one of the Formula One racing drivers wants to trade up."

She hugged him and watched him stride away. At sixty he was still handsome and strong. He had not judged her or made a big fuss. He only ever asked one question in any situation:

"OK - where do we go from here?" so far he had solved every problem in one hell of a life.

As she picked up her mobile to call Judy she heard the beat of the chopper fading as it swung away down the coast. Waiting for the phone to connect she thought on what her father had said. Once she had told Freddie he would understand. She could live this life of glamour, haute cuisine, helicopters and fast boats. She did not have to be breathing in the stench of crime living over a row of shops rattled by 24 hour traffic in Kilburn.

"Anna! Thank goodness you called in - Beaumont has been driving me nuts. Tondelli has really spooked him. He seems to have the idea that your cover has failed and that is why a hard man is there. He reckons you could end up buried at sea," she explained in a concerned voice.

"What's the news on the SIM card?" Anna asked.

"Unbelievable honey - just everyone who is anyone in crooked sport is on Freddie's list. I'm sorry but it does look like your guy is in this up to his neck."

Anna swallowed the news without comment. What did it matter? She was about to jump ship in any case.

"Where does Christine Jones stand?" she asked, aware that she was the key to her survival.

"She's letting it run. She seems prepared to let you see it right through even if there are risks. The phone information will add up to first class evidence - that's all she wants. There's an FBI agent flying in for a conference with her. "

Anna reflected for a second. In the back of her mind she thought of mentioning the white car that had followed Freddie from the heli-port. Deep deep down she knew who it was. She recalled the registration number and decided to let it ride. It was probably too late to change events.

"Thanks for everything Judy. I know you're stuck in the office with Beaumont."

Judy laughed, "Do you think I'd swap my life just to be on a luxury yacht on the Mediterranean having a shagathon with a super hunk?"

"Of course not Judy… it's sheer torture I can tell you." Anna replied, smiling at her friend's assessment of her lifestyle.

"Stay in touch Anna. Beaumont is sure there's gonna be fireworks."

She rang off and sat still for a few moments. Something was wrong. The likes of Scappaticci would not care if Freddie was tied up with some new girlfriend. Only a few people knew her cover story. She would know more soon enough - at least she was sure of that.

She took the chance to clean up and then lay on the bed wrapped in the musky perfume of Freddie's silk ring gown. She would never wash it and never let it go. The strength of the vodka cocktail robbed her of her will. She lay dreamily imagining him pushing inside her, touching nerves deep in her belly that only he had brought alive.. She re-lived his building torrent of tension, feeling her own moistness anticipating his climax. She must have dozed. She awoke to the sensation of soft lips and his breath on her taut belly, his tongue running along the edge of her soft dark forest. A tingle of pleasure ran through her.

"Bonsoir ma belle," he whispered, moving alongside her and resting his cheek on the palm of his huge hand. The other played teasingly down, brushing her soft folded petals that hid her stiffening bud.

"Oh - you're back," she moaned, trying to converse as delicious sleepy warmth began to give way to urgent need. His hand continued with light quicker circles. She turned towards him, offering her breast, pleading silently for him to draw her in to his mouth - to suck her nipple, to pull her pulse of lust through like a Spring shoot pushing up to the light until it burst out into a bloom of love.

At once he picked up her unspoken craving, pulling her in, licking the peak in delicious moist sweeps of his tongue. She wanted to say - wanted to say - wanted to say that she should not just selfishly accept his touch. But now she felt her resolve slipping as if in the distance a sun was rising and rising because it was the nature of the heavens and could not stop.

He brought his lips to hers, caressing her mouth as she peaked into convulsions of wild pleasure.

"My baby - I love you my baby," he whispered as she surrendered to wave after wave of ecstasy.

When he had set her free from the prison of her desire, she sighed and lay back.

"I just get so caught up in the feeling... you just make me come..."

"I feel your rhythms - I am inside you. Believe me - your passion and letting go is my pleasure. This abandon you let me share is your gift as a lover," he murmured, smiling.

She looked back into the warmth of his brown eyes and knew that she had found the home of her soul forever. There would never be another kiss, another touch, another love.

"How was your meeting?" she asked at last.

"Oh - stuff stuff and more stuff. These business guys are just about money," he replied dismissively.

"You like money."

"Sure, perhaps I'm no different. I have a little project - maybe this guy can help."

"Project?" she questioned, only too aware that the word had come up before.

"Yeah - when the fight game is over..."

"He came a long way to find you - he must think it matters," she countered.

He let out a long sigh and lay back on the bed. He closed his eyes, but watched her through one sleepy lid with an expression of desire and tenderness smiling on his lips.

"Nothing matters honey - nothing but us," he mumbled.

She looked at his shoulders, the power of his arms, and the muscled mass of his thighs under his clothing. Love for him swept over her. She unbuttoned his shirt and kissed his chest, flicking open the clasp of his belt. He obliged and wriggled out of his pants as she caressed him, easing down the soft skin over his rock hard tip. He was massive and throbbing, needing and begging for her touch. She bent her head and slipped him into her mouth, tasting the slight musk of pure male.

"Oh my baby - my lover," he groaned.

"My man - my big big man." she whispered, glancing up into his deep brown eyes misted with desire and pleasure.

She wanted this. She wanted this for her own delight and in a way that he would never understand. Never had she given herself in this way, never abandoned her mind to this utter intimacy. His hand ran through her hair, gripping more urgently as she moved her tongue around the rim. She felt him tightening and climbing to a peak and then release helplessly within her, groaning her name in deep grunts of absolute bliss. She thrilled at his free-fall into the warm well of pleasure she had offered, knowing that here in this moment she had surrendered a virginity that no other man had ever known or would ever know.

By 8am they were starving. Freddie dressed in a charcoal jacket, off white linen trousers, a faded blue shirt and decorated cowboy boots - in honor of his American background. With his advice Anna had decided on the mini skirt, red satin blouse and her wrap with high heels. She looked into his tanned face as he kissed her on the deck of the boat. She melted into him, feeling the love of minds expressed in the breath and rhythms of their bodies. She loved him and the turning world curled and folded their love within its heart - maybe for this one last evening. This night she felt it - a premonition that there was not long - but that once a moment is lived and swept away, at least it has been lived and can never be changed.

They walked hand in hand to La Marmite Restaurant in the old town of Antibes. Mike Leyton was already seated. Several diners recognized Freddie and swiveled necks as he crossed the room.

"Mike - we met in Cannes," he opened, shaking her father's hand warmly.

"Mmm - indeed. You only wanted a boat then and now you want my daughter as well! Now that's what I call inflation," he joked.

Anna watched her father's face, knowing that he would be carefully appraising her man and also his likely response to the planned revelations after the sea trial.

"She is so lovely - who could not want her? I think she can stay in the business maybe - I guess you don't want to lose your top executive?" beamed Freddie.

Mike looked a little uneasy. She could see that he did not want to enter the deception further.

"Oh well - we'll see how it goes shall we?" he said breezily.

They dined heartily on sea food specialties de la maison, washed down with an unpretentious crisp Muscadet. Mike did not drink, explaining that he had to chopper back to La Rochelle. The two men formed an instant bond, talking of boats, engines and sea fishing. She had never seen her father so animated and at ease. She was an only child although he had longed for a son. Maybe that is how she ended up as a cop. Maybe now he would have the son or grandson that would make his life... She slapped herself inwardly. That could never be now... now that she had deceived her way into Freddie's heart. A wave of utter sadness rolled in across her.

"Baby - I'm so sorry," began Freddie, "you look so alone there with us guys rattling on about boys toys."

She smiled, putting on her mask of happiness.

"I've got to get airborne," said her father, fixing her with a kind expression but conveying command,"I'll leave everything to you. Deal with every aspect," she was in no doubt as to what he meant.

"Trust me Dad - I won't let you down," she replied, kissing him on both cheeks and letting him go. They sat down while Freddie sipped a cognac.

"Probably my last for a while," he commented with a wry smile, "normally I train for two months."

"It's only a couple of weeks to the fight," she replied, hoping for an insight.

"Yeah - people see me in restaurants and on a boat... they do not see my body... they run off and write that I'm out of shape," he chuckled, looking at her with a wicked gleam in his eye.

"And are you in the right shape?"

"When I step in that ring - I'll do what I have to do," he drawled.

She looked into his exquisite masculine face with the long scar over his brow. She surmised that the good humored chat with her father, the wine and the brandy had opened him up and he wanted to talk.

"And what do you have to do?" she asked, fixing her eyes on his.

"I have to marry the most beautiful woman - that's all that's on my mind."

"God Freddie - why do you shut me out like this?"

"I'm not shutting you out baby," he cajoled, "just think of it as a few minutes of lunacy between now and the rest of our lives."

"Lunacy that could kill..." she pulled up short, not wanting to go there in her own mind or plant the idea in his...

"Anna - I know what I'm doing baby. You just asked your dad to trust you - so do the same and trust your man."

He helped her with her wrap and drew her into his arms, kissing her warmly and searchingly on her lips.

"Allez!" yelled an enthusiastic diner.

He smiled as several females appeared to become motionless staring at him. Anna looked around the room. Then she saw him. Deep in a corner, the guy who had been driving the white car at the helipad. She caught his slow pitiless eye and stared back his menace, recognizing a signal that she had received so many times from dangerous criminals. Abruptly she switched out of her professional character. Perhaps it was already too late and he would have picked up her own cop radar that worked like a dog's nose and would never leave her. At least she knew there were sharks in the water - in case she had to swim.

She took Freddie's arm. She thought deeply about his behavior. Suddenly she realized that above all, he wanted to be seen, wanted to be reported as the playboy champ. Something was cooking and she was sure that Freddie was about to win another Michelin star for cuisine.

The Nereus rocked gently on its moorings. The moon was full and reflected with the harbor lights on the inky water. For a few moments he held her as they stood on the deck taking in the view. He was still and she felt his thoughtfulness as she picked up the slow beat of his heart.

"What are you thinking?" she asked.

"Oh - just how lucky I am to be here with you in this beautiful place. I can smell the salty air, I can know your love and dream of our lives to come. I can look up and wonder at the stars - all those things that not everyone can do. This life is not fair you know..."

She knew he had stopped and did not look at him. Her voice whispered to him in the darkness.

"You seem sad to say that - but it is so. On the streets of the city there are tragedies sleeping in doorways - kids with no chances who die in a despair of drugs - innocent victims of terrible crimes. These things make it more important to see the stars," she replied warmly against his shoulder, sensing that his constantly unspoken sorrow drifted in the still night. She wanted to say more but pulled back, realizing that she was opening up her own inner world that he could never enter.

He shook his head and pulled her to him more firmly.

"You are the strangest creature Anna. You come from a world of wealth and glamour - but sometimes you talk like a social worker."

"Perhaps you don't really know me..."

"You are right," came his deep gentle voice, "we should talk - I should talk. You are to be my wife and there are things - big things you should know."

And there in that moment, looking out into the moonlit velvet darkness she let her secret slip away noiselessly into the ocean and the moment was gone. After the sea trial she would wade straight in. Until then there was love and the warm hard power of her lover to share the night.

Chapter 20

Bertrand and Lucienne served breakfast before setting off for a day shopping in Monte Carlo. Anna wore a simple Leyton marine T shirt and blue cotton shorts. Freddie had opted for jeans and denim shirt.

The twin engines roared into life and soon they were heading out past the Cap D'Antibes, turning east towards Cannes. The Mediterranean sparkled in the warm autumn sun as the Nereus cut through the sea, trailing behind it a path of pure white water like a bridal train. She watched his skill at handling the boat. Everything he did look assured and confident. He checked the depth and radar before pushing the throttles forward. The vessel surged onwards, raising the note from a deep baritone to a clear tenor. They flew and bucked across the tops of waves along the coast. She watched his delighted face as he enjoyed the handling and power of the superb machine. Finally he brought the speed down and headed towards the sea side of the Isle Ste Marguerite, dropping anchor in an area called the Plateau Milieu. He closed down the engines and let the wind and the lapping sea frame the postcard of the Nereus in a pure blue ocean.

Anna went below and returned with a bottle of champagne and two crystal glasses. He had moved to the front deck and was relaxing on the king size white leather sun pad. She sat beside him and bent over, kissing his lips.

"You don't give me a hard sell on this boat," he said, smiling wickedly and running his hand under her T shirt to her aroused longing nipple. His touch was as light as a bird but sent shockwaves vibrating down to the apex of her thighs.

"These boats sell themselves," she murmured, already beginning to twitch at the base of her stomach. She could not control her response to him and knew that her moist heat of desire was rising and opening - shrieking for his touch.

She lay back. Above her was nothing but the infinite blue of the sky and beyond that the invisible universe of stars. They rocked gently on the sea as if she were a cloud, free of the world and all its constraints - free to abandon her body and mind to the ancient gods of lust and desire.

Deftly he raised her shirt and placed his lips in a sweet sucking kiss on her nipple. She felt his hand sweeping teasingly down to the waistband of her shorts and resting on the damp silky barrier of her knickers. Imperceptibly he slipped his finger under the fabric and into her soft lush groove and let out a groan of pure male excitement and arousal.

"Anna - ma belle - je t'aime," he croaked huskily. She let her legs drift apart without modesty as he began his now familiar tiny circles of exquisite teasing. Her nub hardened and screamed for attention as he began to press her little petal folds against some deep focus of joy.

"Oh Freddie - you know you'll make me come.." she whispered in a hoarse lust laden voice that brought a deep animal sound from his throat in response. A warm spill of pleasure began to spread across her belly and thighs. Inside she started to tense and pulse as her mind flooded with the fantasy of his face and the gush of his release, pouring and pouring within her like an unstoppable warm rain.

He continued his delicate caress, his hand between her flesh and her knickers. Her sense of naughtiness and the open air excited her more and more. Now there was only the dark void of pleasure as she released her hold and let the dam of ecstasy burst and gush around her. He felt her convulsion and pressed his lips to her neck, whispering, "You are my woman - I love you so much." His words mixed with the abstract throb of her body and pushed her on to a sensation beyond anything she had known.

She felt him pulling away her shorts and panties and let her thighs open. Her soft longing triangle was exposed to the wild air and sky as she felt his tongue licking down her belly until a jolt of bliss sparked through her as he found her bursting bud. His lips caressed her soft secret folds, teasing and holding her at the brink of oblivion. Her eyes took in the cloudless blue above as he led her on and on towards paradise. Ripples built to waves until the tidal deluge of her abandoned climax swept her away, leaving her powerless to stop, calling his name into space and across the perfect sea.

He felt the tremble of her belly as she came. Now he could no longer control his own desire. He slipped from his jeans letting the power of his erection free. Her wet longing body called to him and drove him forward, desperate to plunge into her,"Je t'aime," he groaned as he slid deep inside, feeling exquisite jolts of pleasure with every move.

She felt him rock hard and massive between her thighs. His thrusts filled and held her open as his gorgeous fullness brought her back to her peak once again. All restraint had drifted away into the wilderness of the sky and sea. She craved for him to come inside her and pulled his iron muscled buttocks towards her as she wrapped her legs around his waist. She could hear his groans lengthening as he plunged to her limits.

He felt her legs wrap around him as the distant drums of his own ecstasy started their unstoppable beat faster and faster. He looked down at her face, soft and enraptured with wordless pleasure. The force of his climax blotted out all thought as his juice rushed and pumped into the moist pulsing heart of his woman - his lover. She let out her own animal squeal of passion and joy and let the pagan spirit of the air and water accept them as two helpless and unashamed creatures of lust and flesh, loving as all time had created them to love.

For a while they lay wrapped in each other's arms, rocked by the motion of the boat. Too soon it began to chill and she watched him as he stirred and made his way back to the controls. His imprint was still warm inside her as the awareness of what had to come dawned on her. As soon as they tied up in the harbor she would tell him - tell him everything. At least he had not learned the truth from some other source. She had to face the truth and her deception. Somehow - somehow she felt that they could still be lovers at bed time.

The engines roared into life and she went to stand behind him as he turned the craft back towards Antibes and opened the throttles. She gently soothed his massive rock hard shoulders, hoping that in some way she could comfort him in advance. The evening was settling as lights began to sprinkle the shoreline of Cannes and the Riviera. A night was coming and could not be avoided.

Skillfully he slid the vessel onto the mooring, shut down the engines and went below as she secured the ropes. She waited for him to return, but he did not appear. She descended the stairs into the saloon where he was sitting silently on the leather sofa looking down at the screen of his mobile. He did not seem to have heard her. Now was the time - she would tell him now...

"Freddie - there has been something - something I should... "

She stopped as his eyes came up to hers. Within them she saw a deep hurt and questioning that she had never seen in the eyes of any man.

"Detective Inspector Leyton... I'm so pleased to meet you," he said sadly but also with a note of ruthless anger.

Her legs almost buckled as she studied his face. He knew. She had hit the wall. Just at the moment when she was going to go for broke he had learned the truth and now he would never believe her. She sensed the cold terrifying anger within him. He remained seated and coiled. In desperation she searched for words, going to him and kneeling. She longed to touch him but held back.

"Metropolitan Police on assignment to Interpol I believe?" he said, shaking his head in disbelief. His deep brown eyes searched into her, willing her to deny it.

"Freddie - I was about to tell you everything... my love... please," she reached out to touch his face. Abruptly he stood up and moved away, leaving her kneeling stupidly on the floor.

His manner was coldly calm. Tears poured down her cheeks. The contrast in their demeanors served to separate her even more from him - from the possibility of explaining to him. If only he would shout or yell. She knew about anger and aggression.

His handsome anguished face stared at her. She sensed a thaw - if only she could get him to listen. She sat down on the sofa and silently questioned his eyes. He answered in a raised voice.

"Tell me - when was I going to know... when I was in jail and you had your next promotion. Would you have fed me some wedding cake through the bars?"

"It's just not like that."

He made a powerful dismissive sweep of his hand.

"Are you trained to have sex with suspects to solve difficult cases?"

"Freddie - I love you... we met by chance... I was afraid you would never want me if you knew I was a cop. Please believe me... please."

She watched him as he paced the saloon. She was acting submissively, as much as anything out of instinct as a police officer. Every word from an angry man is one less ratchet click of tension. She was a proud professional and she loved him. She would let him talk - for now.

"You were selling boats. You must have been following me with a cover story all planned out. Is Leyton Marine just a police front? I cannot believe a man like your father played along. I really thought you guys were for real."

"I am for real and you had better believe that you need me. You are sitting at the table with a mob of killers."

"Did they give you a script Anna? How many lies have there been? If you don't sell boats - who the hell was that little Italian with all those Chinese guys in the hotel in Lyon? I wanted to marry you... I loved you," he stammered.

She let her eyes hold his. He was grabbing at random episodes in their story and not focusing. He was still the same man and she the same woman. He was right to feel betrayed. She could not let his pride destroy their love. For the first time in their relationship she could come out fighting. The big stone of the dishonesty had been lifted from her heart.

"We love each other Freddie. We came together in a crazy way... but we did come together. Are you telling me that you didn't want me... if you hadn't wanted me no police tactic could have made you."

"So the Detective Inspector marries the crook and has his babies... How would that play at Scotland Yard?"

She reflected for a moment, looking at his strong face set in a mask of pain and anger. She had let him have his say. Now she would answer.

"Well - are you a crook? If you are then that's fine with me - I'll be a crook's woman if that's what you want. The Law and the Police can go to hell," she yelled, moving towards him, "are you a crook? Are you? Are you going to throw this fight and take a big wedge from these mobsters? You know what happened to that referee when he wanted to talk to the FBI. I guess you think they wouldn't kill you... Huh... maybe you don't know so much. Maybe you should read some of my files or spend a bit of time in the morgue."

He looked at her as she stood in front of him. A woman so beautiful that she made him ache. A woman with whom he had made love. A woman who had grown to maturity on the streets of South London - who had fronted out violent and desperate criminals and got up the next day to do it all again and again. Her breasts rose and fell as she breathed hard. Whatever became of their lives he could respect her. And desire her. She had at least the strength and defiance of any man he had met in the ring.

"I love you Freddie - right or wrong I love you and yes, I'll have your babies - but in a world that isn't run by low life gangsters. Is that the world you want?"

Despite everything, despite the breaking of her heart, she rejoiced in the freedom to open up and be her true self. She knew he was hearing her words and when the anger had gone he would listen. She clung to that hope as he fired back.

"What I wanted was a woman who told me the truth - not some cynical bitch who would screw her way to promotion."

"Screw! How dare you? We made love Freddie - we made a little corner out of this stinking world and filled it with love and you know that!"

His eyes were as dark as storm clouds. His words hurt deeply yet she kept calm. He clenched and unclenched his huge strong hands in frustration and bewilderment.

"I won't bullshit you Freddie - I was put on your case because I had already met you. I didn't know who you were... I didn't call you for a date. Once the ball was rolling and I was in love with you I couldn't stop because I knew you wouldn't trust me. When you think it through you'll see... please."

And now she could no longer stop the tears. She slumped down on the sofa and let herself cry out the terrible void of emptiness inside her.

She saw him turn and walk to the stairway.

"This is over Anna. I can't ever believe what you say. Even if everything you say is true it's useless if I can't believe it. If some punk hadn't put a note on my website I would have married a cop who was out to lock me up."

Her tears hardened to a sudden anger.

"Who says I was going to lock you up. All I was interested in was the truth about your life. I had to stomach all your little jibes about being a little rich girl. I couldn't blame you for that cos that's all you knew.

"Well what are you then?" he threw back viciously, his handsome face anguished and vulnerable in an expression that made her long to reach out to him.

"I was a spoiled little rich girl who left it all behind to find my own way. You may think you're Mister tough guy but I've seen more bloody violence than you'll ever imagine. I am Detective Inspector Anna Leyton that's what I am and who I am. And I love you with all my heart right or wrong. If you can't see that or have any compassion then you may as well go because you are not the man I believe in."

She was breathing hard, halfway between rage and sorrow. She had said all she could say. He let out a long sigh.

"I loved you and I can't just stop loving you. If I could it would be me who was the fake."

In his eyes she could see his sincerity. The gloves were off and she would not hold back

"Fake... If you are not a fake tell me what the hell is going on?"

She searched his face for the truth. He turned away. She sensed he was on the back foot, wondering how to answer.

"You know nothing of my affairs Anna."

"Then maybe I should. This Scappaticci - this Tondelli - these guys are mobsters. They fix gambling and kill people who get in the way of their greed."

"Really," he exclaimed sarcastically, "it's a terrible world Inspector - the police should do something!"

"Don't be tricky Freddie. I love you but I'm never gonna crawl to these creatures even if you will."

For a fraction of a second she saw a storm of cold dangerous anger flash across his face that almost made her look away but she maintained a hard questioning stare.

"You just don't know anything Anna and now you never will. You are... you were my perfect beautiful woman who is not from my world of compromises, gutters and palaces."

"Huh - nice poetry Freddie, but it's crap."

"Ok - it's all crap. The woman I worshipped and believed in was setting me up and just using me. What makes you better than those crooks?"

She shook her head sadly.

"I think deep down you know that's not me but I don't know how I can ask you to believe it." She croaked as the bitter sorrow of the situation began to seep into her.

"I can't believe anything - it's over," he snapped coldly.

There was something she had to know. Something that could possibly be a matter of life or death.

"Just tell me how you found out," she begged.

"The website - some jerk put on some fan mail."

He looked at the screen of his mobile and read aloud, "Freddie - your black haired Cher ami is on your case. On the pillow tonight is with Interpol by breakfast. When you whisper her name don't forget to call her Inspector."

Her mind hurtled through corridors of questions. The answer was there and she knew it. The informant was too clever for their own good.

His eyes, once again revealing a kindness, were fixed on hers.

"Luckily our gambling friends have not read it. Mom checks everything for spam and trash before it goes out. I have closed down the site for now. I didn't want..."

"You didn't want them to kill me!" she spat.

He nodded.

"If you're just a girlfriend then you're safe. A cop - well - who knows what these guys would do?"

"So you know who they are and what they represent."

"Of course I do Anna," he slammed back at her, "you should scurry back to Scotland Yard while you can."

For one last time she came to him and reached out to soothe his tortured face. She felt the warmth of his skin. This would be the last time she could ever touch him. The thought let go the tears that were massing like troops at the border. He pushed her hand away.

"I'll get my things," he said icily as he turned away.

She did not look up as she heard him come out of the bedroom and go to the bottom of the stair that would take him up on deck and away from her forever.

"I loved you and I will always love you," she said hopelessly.

"Love is about truth Anna. You cannot love a shadow. Loving a shadow is what we call grief," he answered with an obvious catch in his voice.

His words re-opened the gates of her sorrow. She buried her face in her hands and sobbed uncontrollably. Ever since they had met it was going to end this way. She had always known it.

She heard Lucienne talking on the deck and climbed the stairway. She was walking with Freddie towards the car park. She watched as she placed a hand on his shoulder as he got into his car. Then he gunned the Mercedes and was gone.

Lucienne walked slowly back along the pontoon to the boat. The two women embraced.

"He is very bitter and confused. I told him you were about to tell him. Let it all settle Anna - he loves you, even an old woman can see that."

It was comforting to hug Lucienne. She had known her since she was a girl and in many ways she was closer than her own mother.

"What can I do?" she sobbed.

"C'est la vie - crois moi - time will solve it. Let it go for today. Love is a fact like the Eiffel Tower. It is there and just because you are not in Paris it does not mean it fell down."

Anna almost smiled as she kissed her on both cheeks. She thought of the Eiffel tower... so far far away. But standing.

Chapter 21

The Mercedes swallowed the autoroute back to Paris. By the time he swept past the solitary fact of the Eiffel tower his anger had dissipated and his one companion was his loneliness. At the penthouse he lay on the bed, breathing in the perfume of her absence. The most beautiful woman he had ever known was now no more than an empty space in his heart. Someone would pay for this - and he knew exactly where to start.

She lay awake on the soft bed of the luxurious stateroom suite on the Nereus. The gleaming walnut and the sparkling chandeliers seemed to mock her with their irrelevant self satisfied perfection. If there was not love - what was the use of splendor? Mechanically she showered and gasped to see his silk ring robe still lying on the floor. She pulled it to her face and lost herself once again in his scent. At least she had this memento of their love and their union. Finally she fell into an exhausted sleep, wrapped in the flavor and passion of his absence.

It was dawn when she awoke. Footsteps on the deck above - and the tread of town shoes!

A tread that came down the stairs. Her heart pounded. Now she needed to call upon everything she had learned. She pulled the gown around her.

The door opened and a broad silhouette filled the space. She knew at once who it was.

"This had better be important," she spat with a measured insolence.

The figure entered and closed the door with a sinister click. She would later confess to terror but for now she had a job to do.

She flicked on the light. Male, white, 5 feet 9 inches, business suit. The killer -Tondelli.

He sat down at the foot of the bed.

He took in her appearance and nodded as if with approval. She returned the examination - pock marked face, wide gapped stained teeth, merciless reptilian eyes.

Above the background radiation of fear screamed a question - did he know who she was? The next few seconds would tell.

"Pretty lady - such an English Rose," came a mocking gruff response.

"What d'ya want?"

He turned and placed his hand on the bed just a few threatening inches from her knee. He leered with sick smile:

"Just a social call - we are doing a bit of business with Freddie. Looks like he had to shoot off... we worry you know... we worry that a girl like you could be in danger while your man is away."

"You mean danger from you."

"Huh - we're business people - kinda important business. Just tell the champ we called by to make sure you were safe. Maybe we'll call by again. We are all friends - we'll be watching over you honey. I know Freddie would like that."

She looked at his vile fat face. She ached to pull her badge and send him away for the rest of his life. For now he had written a small chapter in his own downfall. She was sure he didn't know who she was. If he did know - she was as good as dead.

"I'll tell him," she replied plainly, coldly imagining him standing in the dock as she gave her evidence.

Tondelli stood and once again appraised her. He crudely cupped his groin with a hand bearing a selection of crass gold rings.

"Bye for now pretty lady," he growled.

She shuddered as he went to the door and was gone. She heard his tread on the deck and lay back with a sigh of relief.

That was close!

Her thoughts raced through the labyrinth of her situation. Obviously Freddie had not played ball exactly as they had wanted. The image of his face forced its way into her mind. He had gone. He had shown her a dream of a different life but now she was awake and it was the cold dawn. No one knew that they had split - and she was not about to inform her bosses at Interpol. She was a cop and this was her case. She would cling to that.

Detective Inspector Anna Leyton turned to the question of the website fan mail that had betrayed her. The words "Black haired Cher ami," echoed in her head and the echo rolled back across several years until it bounced back at full volume. She knew the answer and now there was the small matter of proving it.

Chapter 22

The Air France jet climbed away from Nice as she settled back with a glass of Bordeaux. She wondered if the flight-path would take her over Paris. Being away from him at least allowed her to stand back and think about him clearly.

Okay - he was World champion. All the Press was screaming that he was out of shape. She was no judge but he sure didn't look out of shape. The more they told the tale of his expected defeat, the more money poured on to Brennan.

If a punter backed Freddie he could now get good odds. What if he wasn't out of shape? What if he wanted to be seen in London and Paris with a girl on his arm? Why had the paparazzi homed in on him so easily to fuel the press stories? Why was he apparently happy to mix it with a slugger like Brennan who was obviously a tool of criminals? And one big big question. A question that had gnawed at her every moment. What was the sadness at the heart of his soul - that black door that he kept locked behind his masculine beauty? What was it that she had seen in the tears in his deep brown eyes and that she had longed to know?

As she thought she felt the pricking heat of her own tears stinging behind the lids of her closed eyes. Somewhere beneath the plane he was living under the same sun and despite everything that had happened she knew that their love stood as bold as the Eiffel Tower.

She glanced out the window as the aircraft lined up from the North to head in to Heathrow. The Thames, New Scotland Yard and the Houses of Parliament featured as toys in a model landscape. She was home and it was time to work.

She took the tube to Queen's Park. She needed to speak to Judy. She was the one person with whom she would trust the truth.

"I'm home," she said as Judy answered the phone.

"God Anna - I've been frantic. Beaumont is sure that your cover has been blown. He says he saw an entry on Freddie's website - but now no one can access the site. He says Tondelli will kill you."

"It's under control. Freddie found out who I am - we've split up Judy but no one else must know. I want to stay close to him."

As she spoke her emotions started to overwhelm her. The sudden end of her dreams, the brush with Tondelli. She longed for Freddie's fearless protective arms around her.

"But if they find out - if Freddie or Mom tells them," gasped Judy.

"Then I'll face it. I know he won't betray me to them. I don't think he is cooperating."

"But there is money pouring on Brennan to win. This fight will launder half the dirty loot on the planet. We are tracing the credit cards Anna! You can't go on closing your eyes to the truth. These crooks must believe he's in their pocket - we are talking millions here. He hasn't trained for the fight… you know that. He's been wandering around the South of France with a girl on his arm. It's like he has some kinda death wish…"

Anna reflected on everything her friend was saying. She meant well and she would not clash with a dear old friend who only had her best interests at heart.

"I love him and I believe in him. I'm gonna stay with him at all costs."

She could feel the silence at the other end of the line.

"Did you get to keep the ring?" Judy asked with a change of mood back to her normal cheerful cynicism at all things human.

"It's on a chain round my neck. I'll show you Monday morning at the office," she replied warmly, "there's a lot to talk about."

She called Freddie and let it ring out. Then she called again. Then she sent a text to go with all the others, "Good or bad - je t'aime pour toujours jusqu'à la mort."

And it was true - this was her love and if need be she would die for it.

Chapter 23

She was at her desk by eight o'clock. She had chosen her smartest deep gray business suit. Her hair shone and her lips glossed in a passionate red. She checked her look in the mirror - her bright white teeth, her flawless skin. The diamond Cartier ring nestled between her breasts secured on a silver chain. She thought of him and of what he faced. He had not replied to her messages. She guessed that by now he was in Monterey California, consulting with Mom and training for the show-down with Brennan.

Judy hurtled into the office like a subway train squealing into the station.

"God - had to leave the babe with Brian - his mum's overdone the curry and can't get off the toilet!"

Anna smiled warmly. For all her own troubles and the cut and thrust of international crime - real everyday life went on with all its comedy.

"So - you propose putting your head right in the lion's mouth by jetting out to California," commented Judy, placing two cups of hot coffee on the desk and raising an incredulous eyebrow, "baby - someone knows who you are! We don't know who... but how well can you float with a few bricks in your sack. Do you want to see the FBI files on these thugs?"

"I know who it was," Anna replied, watching her friend's face, wondering if she could accept the truth.

"Well who?"

"It really is best that you don't know... "

"You're joking... how could that be?"

"Politics and survival Judy. If I'm wrong I don't want you out of the Force driving an all night taxi-cab to bring up your kids."

"Eh?

"Trust me. I have a plan."

Judy shrugged her shoulders uncertainly.

"You're gonna need one I think. Oh by the way, a couple of Kilburn cops breezed in to see you about a guy called Pete Making," Judy added.

Anna let out a sigh and shook her head wearily.

"Tondelli... I know it was him who killed him."

God Anna - do you know about all this? He was shot dead not far from where you live... Anna - are you ok with this stuff? If you have a lead on this case you have to come clean."

Anna thought quickly. Her friend was right. It was her duty to tell all she knew.

"Look - if I say anything now I'll never get the go ahead to stick with Freddie and that's all that matters. These crooks want me alive as a lever to keep him on-side. As it stands I'm just ahead of the hounds but I have to keep running."

Judy shook her head slowly.

"I'll do what I can for you Anna you know that - but you're kinda beyond Earth orbit."

Anna reached out and squeezed her shoulder.

"Trust me. It'll come good," she said.

The Monday conference came to order, but not before Deputy Assistant Commissioner Christine Jones had embraced Anna in front of everyone.

"A major Interpol success - the contact list from La Salle's phone links all the main players," she beamed.

Commander Beaumont Locke remained seated, shuffling his papers and clearing his throat with a dramatic impatience. Finally he began.

"Let's begin with reports from you humble stay-at-home plods and then perhaps the star of Interpol can entertain us with her Continental and Mediterranean adventures," he boomed in a sarcastic tone."

Christine Jones shot him a glance of pure venom but kept quiet. A succession of analysts gave their reports. About sixty million dollars had been placed on Brennan to win the fight. Most of this cash was linked to organized crime. Just as Freddie's form appeared to be at its lowest several millions had gone on him to win.

"What is that all about?" asked Judy, picking up an intuitive glance from Anna.

"These are mug punters. They're the kinda folk who'll go for a bet just because it offers a big win. The bookies love these guys," quipped the analyst.

Anna thought it over. What if Freddie wanted the odds against him?

"But could La Salle win?" she asked disingenuously.

Commander Locke let out an exasperated sigh and looked up at the ceiling.

"La Salle is consorting with mobsters Inspector!"

"Perhaps our colleague can give his own view," said Anna with a defiant stare.

"Er... well, yes he could win. But the pro gamblers are not fools. He has never won by a knockout. Without training he could not go the distance for a win on points. It looks like this is a final pay day and that he can't be bothered."

Anna nodded. There was no fault in the logic. Beaumont Locke was speaking.

"So finally - may I describe it as the climax of our conference - Inspector Leyton will get up close and personal and report direct from ringside. Let us hope she will speak in English - not all of us have her education."

"I'm sure she will dumb it down to your level," snapped Christine Jones with a wink at Anna. A ripple of awkward laughter ran around the room.

She gave her report in a matter of fact tone. Apparently he had done no training - he had met with Scappaticci in Antibes - he appeared to have money to burn. When she laid out the bare facts she had to admit that he looked pretty shady. She was about to wrap it up when she found herself saying

"My gut feeling is that he not a crook. He is a complex and cultured man. My assessment is that he is playing them along."

It was a stupid thing to say. But he was her lover and she would love him for the rest of her life and defend him.

"Gut feeling Inspector," sneered Beaumont with a theatrical weariness.

Anna ignored him. She had left out a few little facts such as Freddie's ring snuggled in her cleavage and the visit from Tondelli.

"We should all congratulate Anna on obtaining his contact list," interjected Christine Jones, "we are building up a picture of conspiracy and this is a vital part of the story. You must tell us how you did it one day."

"What about the website entry - someone blew Anna's cover and we ought to know who," said Judy suddenly.

"We'll never know that. Could be anyone - wasn't he photographed with some girl in London? Wasn't you was it Inspector?" said Beaumont with narrowed serpent eyes.

"The website has closed - so we can assume that the webmaster of the site did not want the information to come out," added Christine.

"The webmaster is Mom - once I get to her we'll know more," Anna breezed, watching Beaumont's face twist into a depiction of rage.

"You cannot be planning to take this any further?" he snapped.

Anna glanced at Christine who gave a subliminal flick of an eyebrow in her direction.

"Let's button up for now. I've got a meeting with the minister about illegal meat imports - foot and mouth and fascinating things you don't want to know about dried elephant flesh. The three of us will meet in your office at 11 o'clock Beaumont."

With that the meeting was over and Anna scrambled away to her own territory. Judy slumped down at her desk.

"There'll be tears before bed time. You simply cannot go out to California when you know that our friend Tondelli would wipe you out without a look back."

Anna thought of Freddie, hardly aware that Judy had spoken. She imagined his smooth powerful body, the depth in his brown eyes, the sensation of his lips on her skin.

"Hey - Dolly daydream!"

"I'm sorry..."

Then from nowhere the tears began. He was no longer hers - it was no good to pretend.

"I love him so much - I need him so much. He's in danger too isn't he?"

Inside she felt as if she had turned to cold stone and that even that was splitting in two.

"What can you do Anna - except float around as bait for the sharks? You can't tell the bosses that in a week you have got engaged to and split up from the target."

She thought for a minute. She hadn't begun to think it through. She needed a big lie.

"I've been invited to meet Mom... um... I didn't tell the conference because the Judas might be one of the team. Mom is thinking about a boat charter business working out of Monterey. Yeah - Leyton Marine could lease her a couple of boats and if the clients wanted to buy at the end of the charter we could fix a commission for her. How's that for a deal?"

She laughed at her own deviousness.

"I'd hate to have you as an enemy Anna. You make Machiavelli look like Santa Claus."

"And talking of Machiavelli... we need to get a move on!"

Anna opened her laptop and started to change all her passwords. Then she copied all files onto a spare hard drive. Judy watched curiously.

"OK - I've just gotta ask what you're doing?"

"Look - I'm gonna swap laptops with a suspect that's all."

"Suspect?"

Anna nodded as a revelation began to sink in. Judy looked incredulous.

"Beaumont - you are going to steal a police commander's laptop because you think he put the tip on the website! Anna... you had better get this right. These machines are encrypted... how can you get into the hard drive? He won't have just left it in a file."

"I can't get into it - but I hope I know a woman who can," replied Anna with a steely smile.

"You're risking everything Anna. Everything! You've met some guy and you have lost the plot honey. God - why couldn't it be me?"

Anna laughed and took a deep breath. Everything was only one thing - and he was on the other side of the Atlantic.

Christine Jones sat next to Anna. She was an upright woman, strangely handsome and aristocratic. She wore a rather dated woolen trouser suit with a white shirt and Hendon police college honors graduate tie. Her graying hair was neatly bobbed and her hazel eyes hinted at a quick intelligence more than kindness.

"You look so beautiful Anna. I'm so proud of your work on this case."

Commander Locke smiled through gritted teeth. Christine was well aware of his tension and was obviously enjoying the tease.

"So - can we get you to the States? You'd be undercover without a safety net."

"It's out of the question. The likes of Tondelli may have found out who she is," insisted Beaumont.

"Police work is not without its dangers Commander. It's not just about management training, knighthoods and pensions you know," smiled Christine, twisting a knife into a soft spot.

"I've been invited to speak to Mom about a lease deal on a couple of boats," Anna said plainly. Her heart was pounding. She just had to pull this off.

Beaumont looked up at the ceiling as if appealing for divine help. Anna took the chance to spot his lap top under his desk and slid hers alongside as if she was merely putting it down. From the corner of her eye she caught Christine's questioning glance and a slight nod. She knew what she was doing. The Blue Witch! She knew!

"Well - Bravo! That'll do nicely," exclaimed Christine.

"I can't believe I'm hearing this," Beaumont stuttered.

"I believe I head the Interpol bureau Commander... the Home Office is very keen to see democratic British police on a world stage. Fighting the causes of crime in every dark corner of Tyranny; extending ideas of justice, freedom and democracy to the people of the world. Did you hear the minister's recent speech Beaumont?"

"Of course."

"That's settled then. Lunch at the House of Lords so must dash," announced Christine standing up.

Anna bent down and collected the laptop without a blink. Her heart thumped. She was a cop and a professional. All the same pulling a stunt on another officer hurt - even though it was Beaumont. Risking an undercover colleague out of personal spite was a low as you could go. They all lived by the same code.

She turned and walked from the office. Once outside she looked at Christine, remembering that this woman was a Deputy Assistant Commissioner of Scotland Yard who had just seen her pull a swap on a police Commander's laptop.

"Get going Anna - get out of the building. You have my number - call me in 20 minutes," she whispered. She half ran to her office.

"Judy - get me booked on any flight to LA or San Fran. Call me with details. If anyone wants me tell them I've gone sick with a migraine."

She made for the door. Suddenly she turned back to look at her poor bewildered friend once again left with all the unglamorous mess and trouble.

"When this is over I'll make all this up to you Judy - I promise."

"Don't be so soft - just come back."

The two women embraced and parted. Now there would be fun!

Once clear of the building Anna made for the Tate Gallery on the embankment. She knew the steps would be crowded and she could see anyone approaching long before anyone could spot her. She just hoped he had used this laptop. He was a useless cop. So he had seen the website entry had he? How odd - it had never gone out live!

She took out the business card Christine had given her and called the number.

"Great minds think alike my dear," said Christine

"What?"

"I thought the same darling - but I didn't quite have the balls to nick the evidence. I have a squad set up and running on this little matter but it looks like you've jumped the gun."

Anna gasped. Just what did this woman know? How bloody ruthless was she?

"Can we meet on the steps of the Tate?"

"I can see you already," replied Christine, "I need a smoke - just stay where you are."

Anna watched as an official black Jaguar pulled up. Christine stepped out and watched the car speed away along Millbank towards Parliament Square. She lit a cigarette and climbed the steps.

"I've got a friend popping over to meet us. We could get a coffee."

"Popping over?"

"From across the river darling."

Across the river rose the famous modern headquarters of the Secret Intelligence Service - MI6.

"James Bond?"

"Jane Bond actually - a wonderful young gal - and a very close friend."

Anna took in the meaning. This was unreal. She was at the brink of another world of wonderful seductive power.

The older woman offered her arm for Anna to take.

"I'm harmless you know - but I won't deny a taste for rare beauty," she said urbanely as they walked into the gallery as if walking arm in arm with such a woman was the most natural thing in the world.

They sipped coffee. Christine looked over her cup raising an eyebrow.

"How did you know it was Beaumont?"

"It's in his kiss," joked Anna.

"That's where it is!" sang Christine with a conspiratorial smile of understanding.

"The Cher song... the website entry used the word 'Cher'. The first time I ever met him he tried to make a little joke about me being 'my dear' - 'Cher'- in French - because of my long dark hair. I guess he didn't remember."

"Huh - he never was much of a cop. We used to say he couldn't detect a gas leak with a box of matches!"

Anna smiled.

"How did you know?"

"Gut feeling - my guess is that he thought he would just blow you out with La Salle. He didn't want you killed. It was just spiteful ex lover stuff. When he learned a real killer like Tondelli was on that plane into Nice he went to pieces. When he said he'd seen the website entry I knew it was the old trick of stealing your wallet then helping you look for it."

Just then Christine stood up and greeted a young woman with a kiss on the lips. Anna stood and shook hands, quickly taking in a beautiful coltish girl of about twenty seven with a riot of auburn curls. Her slightly freckled face was fresh and shrieked English upper class. She wore a pink silk blouse open sufficiently to reveal ample milky white breasts. So this was a spy! There was something about this girl that even made Anna aware of the innocent sexuality of a woman. Something about the soft tempting blossom of a female, some hint of what a man would feel - what Freddie would feel for her.

"This is a police encrypted laptop - we need to decode the hard drive," breezed Christine.

"What about passwords?" asked Anna naively.

The girl smiled.

"We don't knock at many front doors," she said in a slightly patronizing accent.

Anna nodded. This woman was from a place with different rules. Her mind flipped to Freddie. Somewhere he was alive, transmitting his aura...

Then the girl was gone and Christine was phoning her driver.

"I'll call you as soon as we have the information. Keep yourself out of reach. I've got this wretched meeting at the House of Lords. The minister fancies me as a law and order battle axe on the red benches - Baroness of Streatham or some such."

She was amazing. They hugged and Christine strolled away to her waiting Jaguar, pulling hard on yet another Marlboro.

For a moment she paused on the steps. All around young students spilled out like pots of paint on a canvas of stone. All those strangers - all those unknown lives of birthdays, tragedies, tattoos, ambitions and regrets. Here in this circus only she knew the depth of her desolation and her fear for what the future held.

Chapter 24

It was rush hour on Oxford Street when Christine called. If she was going to California to meet Mom and watch a World title fight she would need to be dressed. Anna listened to the news transfixed.

"It's all on there Anna. The day after you went to Paris he placed that message. We have had a discussion and he has gone. The minister has offered him a safe parliamentary seat. Beaumont has made a press release telling a grateful public that he intends to bring his experience to the Palace of Westminster. There's a by-election next month for some spot near Manchester. All it needs now is for the voters to share his own opinion of himself."

"It all seems incredible," she stammered.

"Just be careful Anna - you'll be flying in under the radar and we may not be able to see you. Keep your head - this is not a Mills and Boon novel."

"I'm just a girl selling boats," she began.

"And I'm the sugar plum fairy," laughed Christine, "I don't care how we get these thugs locked up so I'm not going to ask you too many questions. Just for now I'm not gonna ask how some dead reporter has your number... I expect you to stand by your man - he's not our target honey."

Anna gulped. So she knew about the poor little guy shot dead in Kilburn.

"Chris - look, that reporter..."

"Ciao Anna," Christine interrupted, "I'm on top of all that - just pull this one off for us ok. I'll look after all the local stuff."

Anna took the tube from Oxford Circus back to Queens Park. Once home she poured a large glass of wine but set it aside. She dressed herself in Freddie's gown and the Cartier ring on the chain around her neck. She opened her e-mail. A message from Judy set out her travel schedule. Police driver pick up at 11.30 to Heathrow Terminal 5. Flight, British Airways 0287 to San Francisco. Driver will have dossier of all known addresses and contacts including an assigned FBI agent - John Mayer. Local flight to Monterey. Room booked at the Monterey Bay Inn, Cannery Row.

Judy worked so hard and all that with two kids to bring up. When all this was over she would not forget her friend.

She picked up the wine but hesitated. A thought she dare not think, a thought somehow burrowed inside her flashed across her mind. Best leave the wine - you never know.

Then she sent a reckless text,"I love you my bull and my poet! I'm coming to find you. If you never want to see me again just ask the boys to kill me - I won't be hiding."

She stabbed the send button and folded herself up on her lonely bed. The message zipped away into space - but at least it had left her heart. The heavy male perfume of the robe aroused her but brought no desire for completion. It would merely amplify her loneliness. She longed for him inside her. She recalled how he had thrust into her just three days ago on the deck of the boat. She had been wild and carefree. There was only a small chance of pregnancy. She turned her face into the fabric of the gown and let her tears mix with the musk of his body. And so what if she had fallen for his child? They would be linked and his baby would look to her face for love and draw life from her breast. In her turmoil she could not tell if she wanted such a problem or not.

As she drifted into sleep she saw his face. The kind gentle eyes that she had seen brim with tears at some secret sorrow. She would not be much of a detective if she could not at least unlock this mystery.

Chapter 25

On the flight she had the chance to study the dossier. Her attention shot to the phone number and address in Pacific Grove for Mrs. Linda La Salle. Somehow she was going to have to get through the natural hostility of this woman. She had deceived her son and made a fool of him. She had no right to expect any cooperation even if Linda La Salle was not herself a crook who would exploit her own son out of greed.

She opened a copy of 'The Ring' magazine she had bought at the airport. She had a growing fascination with the awful spectacle of boxing. It contained a courage and nobility that normal life could not expose. Not everyone was a world champion. Many were just beaten up and thrown away. On page 2 there was Freddie! He was standing on the middle rope, arms raised in victory. A photo of Billy 'The Boulder' Brennan appeared in the next column. His face was battered and his blue eyes looked cruel and merciless. His shoulders were wide and one showed a tattoo of a naked girl holding a pit bull dog on a chain.

The article recycled tales of Freddie being out of shape, consorting with a girl in the South of France just two weeks before the fight. How on Earth did they know this kind of stuff? The article concluded with the words, "Perhaps it would have been better for the Frenchman to tend his grapes rather than confront the wrath of Brennan. He will need every minute at Pete's gym in Seaside CA if he is to stand a chance on the big night in New York. Both men will enter the ring undefeated. Who would ever have thought that you could get odds of 5:1 for the Champion to lose?"

She touched his glossy photo as tears once again filled her eyes. Somewhere he was living and breathing. Could she transmit her love to him - could he feel her love as she hung in the sky seven miles above the Atlantic holding his picture?

She picked up a hire car from the Avis desk at Monterey airport. She should have just taken a compact but instead drove away in a Crossfire convertible. She had dreamed of driving by the Pacific Ocean with Freddie on Highway One with the wind in her hair. Now she had only dreams. She was an emptiness defined by his absence. She checked in at the Monterey Bay Inn on Cannery Row. She sent him a message, "Love you. Will dream of you," and slept wrapped in his robe as the sea lions barked on the harbor breakwater.

Chapter 26

In the morning she called her FBI contact - Special Agent John Mayer. Twenty minutes later a square cube of a guy strolled into the lobby. He was about forty with fair crew-cut hair. He had an easy laid back smile.

Anna had dressed in cream linen trousers with a short coral colored tailored jacket over a floral scoop necked blouse. She knew at once he was a cop and stood to greet him.

"Pleasure to meet you," he said with a rigid politeness and a firm handshake, "I kinda guess I'm here to stop you ending up in the ocean."

"You're my guardian agent then," she said with a warm smile that she could see slightly embarrassed him. She could feel he had not expected this. This was a one woman guy and she was at home. They took a seat in the lounge and ordered coffee.

"I have to explain some rules Anna. You have no powers here. You are a civilian helping the police - if you can."

She nodded her understanding.

"May I ask - um - what is your relationship with La Salle?"

"I'm his fiancée, but that's between us," she answered feeling the sting of the lie in her heart.

Agent Mayer raised an eyebrow. Clearly it was not normal for an undercover cop to be engaged to a suspect. He shook his head a little before speaking.

"Well, like I say ma'am - keep in touch. There are guys high above me who want this to run. Don't take any risks - these crooks have no respect for a woman. I guess you'll be checking out - um - Freddie."

"Well not so much. He's in final training and it's not - you know - a girl thing."

He smiled a little.

"Kinda keeping his strength for the fight..."

"Quite so. Quite so," replied Anna with a deliberate Englishness.

"Hey - you really are a Mary Poppins," laughed Mayer, visibly relaxing, "so tell me - what is your guy up to? I'm a wrestler, not that WWF stuff but real grappling ma'am."

Anna smiled broadly. She liked this guy.

"What's he up to?" she repeated.

"Yah - you know - Freddie always goes the distance - he's no big puncher. We guess the referee will let Brennan fight 12 rounds with his head in Freddie's face. Billy Brennan is one tough psycho and on home ground you can't see any other winner. The question is why La Salle agreed to this fight in New York? It's got to be just about money."

Anna thought quickly. It would be a strange fiancée who did not believe in her man.

"He's gonna win. I only know what Freddie tells me and I know he is confident," she said, glad that she was not telling a lie.

"That's great - I'll tell my wife Jo to book that cruise to Europe. I can get five to one on Freddie and a tip from Mary Poppins is good enough for me."

"Don't risk too much..."

"Hey - we're cops Anna. Risk is something else for us."

She beamed. It was good to have the companionship of a fellow officer.

"Just don't sell the house."

Agent Mayer stood up and shook hands again.

"Stay in touch. As far as I can see you should be safe. We won't be following you so report anything unusual. Like I say - you're a tourist so enjoy Monterey."

Anna thanked him and watched him go. He was as broad as a barn door. If it came to any situation she would want him on her side. For now it was a beautiful day and she was a girl on a mission.

As she reached her car she saw some kind of paper under the wiper. Surely she hadn't got a parking ticket! She picked it up and read a note typed in large print -

WELCOME TO MONTEREY. SAY HI TO YOUR MAN AND TELL HIM TO BE A GOOD BOY.

She swiveled round half expecting to find somebody there. She should tell guardian agent Mayer but the result would be her removal from the case. She was bait in a trap that she had set herself. The spring was winding up and getting ready to snap.

In the harbor sea lions barked and a hint of clam chowder drifted on the ocean breeze. She started the Crossfire and gunned the throttle South towards Pacific Grove. Mom owned a neat little $4 million house in Acropolis Street between the Ocean and the golf course. She cruised by and parked out of sight. A Toyota SUV was on the driveway. She had wanted to see the house but did not intend to provoke some kind of drama on the doorstep. She called the number from the dossier.

"Hi - what's up?" answered a confident female voice.

Anna's heart raced. This would not be easy.

"Linda La Salle?"

"Who wants to know?"

"My name is Anna - Anna Leyton."

"You've got some nerve young woman!"

"Mrs. La Salle - I know I made mistakes..."

"Mistakes! You rip my boy off for a twenty thousand dollar Cartier ring while you're trying to get him in jail?"

"I love him. I can't live without him. You can have the ring now if it's just about the money."

"Now, waddayamean. Now! Are you in town? Where the hell are you? Just leave us alone."

Anna struggled to suppress her emotions. She could tell this woman was as hard as stone. She tried a different approach.

"You know he's in danger from these gangsters - Scappaticci and Tondelli. I know who they are and I guess you do too. Freddie was never the police target. I may not have told him everything but perhaps he didn't tell me the whole truth either."

She sensed that something she had said had hit a softer spot. Linda La Salle answered abruptly.

"Just stay out of our hair. We don't want you here."

"Has Freddie said that?" Anna asked desperately.

Linda snapped a final, "Goodbye," and hung up. Anna rested her head on the steering wheel and could no longer hold back her tears. What was she doing here? What did she hope to achieve. It was not about police work. It was about her man. The most likely result of her activities would be a visit from the boys. The note on the windshield had hinted that he was not cooperating. She was their key to him. At least he would know one day that she had loved him.

She heard the sound of approaching footsteps. She checked the mirror anxiously. It was only a slim female jogger who slowed briefly to look at her before crossing the street and turning the corner. She was getting jumpy.

She drove down to the beach and looked out at the azure, turquoise and aquamarine cocktail of the Pacific Ocean. Waves split into pure white fragments against an off shore rock. The beautiful loneliness of the scene mirrored her feelings of desolation. The rollers finished their journey pounding their force against the uncaring sand. She lay her head back and let a wave of fantasy break over her as he kissed her lips and moved inside her. For a few seconds he was there again in her heart but too soon the image washed away leaving only the call of gulls and the trickle of her desperate tears.

She headed back through Monterey to Seaside and parked up across the street from Pete's run-down gym. A yellow painted door appeared to open onto stairs that led up to a room above a Laundromat. She watched a couple of tough looking Hispanic guys bundle laughing out of the door and stroll to an impossibly battered pick-up. They roared away as an old Camaro growled slowly past. The driver sported shades and a bandana. Did he look back at her in his mirror? She couldn't be sure.

She crossed the street and pushed the button on a ragged intercom. She stood feeling out of place on the street as a group of kids with backward baseball caps slouched by. She caught an eye contact of insolence.

"Yah?" said a rough voice from the speaker.

"Is Freddie there?"

"Who are ya?"

"Anna."

"Wait."

She waited. The old Camaro growled another length of the street. She was edgy.

"Nope - he ain't here," snapped the intercom.

"Tell him I've got a message from Tondelli - tell him Anna loves him! Geddit!" she half shouted at the seedy chipped door.

A reply crackled out, "Yeah."

She crossed back to the car, hit the soft top control and took off South towards Highway One with her raven hair streaming back in the wind like the tail of a galloping horse. Nothing had surprised her. She had not expected Linda La Salle to welcome her to her home or to be offered the red carpet at Pete's gym. At least they all knew she was here. Stage one was over. Stage two was for another day.

Chapter 27

The first gray light of dawn was in the sky as she walked from the hotel down to the path that ran along the coast. Dressed in trainers, jogging bottoms and her Bench top she began to run back towards Pacific Grove. The smell of salt and fish filled her lungs. A big black guy on skates startled her as he powered noiselessly along the path. There was no one else in sight. She ran on, straining her eyes into the distance. Then she saw a figure ahead - a jogger approaching. She pulled up her hood watched for a minute before turning and running away in the same direction - but at a far slower speed. This was a wild guess…

The sound of footsteps came closer and closer behind her. She did not turn. It was a powerful runner and she could hear his breathing. He was right on top of her now! He was moving alongside... She heard his startled exclamation as he pulled up.

She span round and searched into his deep brown eyes and handsome face for a glimmer of hope - of love.

"Freddie!" she gasped.

He stared at her. Her heart leapt. She was within reach. He took a step and pulled her into his arms as her tears of joy poured down her hot cheeks. His strong contoured arm curled around her waist while he pushed back her hood and gently traced the line of her jaw towards her lips.

"Anna!"

She could hear the emotion in his voice as he lifted her from the ground and pressed his lips to hers in a tender kiss. She melted into the hardness of his body, feeling her strength flowing out of her. She felt his grip relax and she found herself standing in front of him.

"This can never work," he said with a shake of his head.

"Tell me you don't still love me and I'll go," she sobbed angrily.

"Are you still on my case Detective?"

"I'm on the case - these guys have got at least sixty million dollars to gain if you lose this fight. They won't let you freestyle through this. Tondelli paid me a visit before I left Antibes..."

"God Anna... I didn't want you mixed up in this."

"But I am!"

"You could have walked away - stayed in London. You're putting your head in a noose here."

"You're my man Freddie. My man."

He let out a deep sigh. She searched his expression, gazed at his lips, brushed her eyes along the savage scar above his eye.

"I'm gonna win this fight Anna - there's things you can't hope to understand at present - maybe I should have told you..."

He stopped and steadied his gaze on her face. The warmth and nobility of the man shone out from his passionate eyes. She felt his desire for her as he pulled her to him again, cupping her soft butt with his powerful hand. She felt the thrill of her flesh against his hard body. He tilted her chin up and found her lips. She lost herself in his kiss as his love and passion poured into her. He rocked her gently in his arms as the world with all its troubles slipped away.

"I'm late for breakfast and a day at the office," he said with a smile, "you'll get a call in a while - I'm going to do something I should have done..."

He stopped and studied her, "I understand how your father got involved in this - I really do."

She smiled back despite her tears. The big skater swept past on his return journey.

"Keep your phone on. Just wait for a call," he said as he accelerated away with the grace and power of a tiger along the path towards Seaside. She watched him until he was a dot in the distance. Her lover. Her man.

She jogged back to the hotel - singing.

"You're cheerful," commented the receptionist.

"It's the Eiffel Tower - it didn't fall down yet!" she replied to the confused girl with a laugh.

She phoned agent Mayer with nothing to report. He sounded bored.

"Okay ma'am - you have a nice day."

She intended to.

Chapter 28

It was 10.30 when the phone rang. Anna knew the voice at once.

"You'd better get over here - you're probably staked out watching me anyway. This ain't my idea young woman."

"Thank you for seeing me..."

"Save it Honey! Let's get this done."

She had already dressed in a somber gray trouser suit and medium heeled shoes. Half an hour later she swung the car onto Linda La Salle's driveway in Pacific Grove. The front door of the beautiful detached house was glazed. She took a deep breath knowing that this would not be easy. As she approached she saw a figure already behind the door poised to open it. Anna reached out to shake hands. The older woman ignored the gesture and moved aside.

"You're only here because Freddie wants it this way," she snapped icily.

The house smelled pleasantly of sandalwood and coffee. Anna followed through a large hallway and climbed a wide marble stairway to the first floor. Evidently the floors were inverted with the lounge area above the bedrooms. As she stepped into the room she could see why. The whole end wall was a window looking out over the Pacific Ocean.

"Wow!" Commented Anna involuntarily.

"Let's hope you don't put us in jail so we can enjoy it."

Anna bit her tongue. At least she was here. She studied her adversary - a woman of about fifty two, mid brown shoulder length hair expensively and flawlessly dyed. She wore a smart pink cardigan tied under her breasts. Her neat gray trousers were well cut and showed off her pert - probably personal trainer honed butt. Her face was almost beautiful with an aristocratic fine long nose. Her plucked eyebrows arched cynically over her green cattish eyes.

"Coffee?"

"Thanks."

"Freddie is my son. I know you know that but you cannot possibly be too aware of that. He has risked his life and brains to be where he is. Don't think I take it for granted."

"He loves you."

Linda La Salle threw back her head with a cold laugh -

"Well thanks for letting me know about my own son - that's not too bad when you've only known him for a week."

Anna watched her face. She knew enough of Linda La Salle's past to realize that she had passions of her own.

"There's little I can say to please you. I want to be friends but if your mind is made up I may as well say nothing," she replied firmly.

Linda nodded and took a sip of coffee with a slight knowing smile. The way to deal with Linda La Salle's serve was to come straight into the net and volley!

"That was a neat trick this morning," she said, holding Anna's eyes in a steady gaze.

"Trick?"

Linda laughed openly, revealing perfect teeth.

"Look - the poor guy thinks you just happened to be out jogging and he just happened to catch you up. He's a man for Pete's sake - he has no idea how devious we women can be."

"You should have told him," Anna fired back.

"What - and spoil all his fun? I knew some heartless bitch would teach him soon enough."

"Let's hope I'm around to save him if she shows up."

Anna watched as Linda reflected a little. Ten years of police work had sharpened her counter punching. She decided to take the initiative.

"I know what you think of me - but I love him. I had already met him by chance before I knew who he was. I'll tell you how everything happened and it's up to you what you believe."

Linda listened and let her relate the whole story. Finally she ended saying,

"I had never loved a man before - not truly loved. I'm not some stupid wannabe who's never seen an angry man. City streets are unforgiving places. I'm a cop because I don't want the thugs to rule the world. I'm not proud of myself but I'm proud to be a police officer."

For a few moments Linda La Salle sat silently. Her eventual response took her by surprise.

"And you're here - even though that slug Tondelli would kill you. You do know that Anna don't you."

"I know it - but they don't know who I am."

"But you knew I could have told them - and you still went ahead without knowing."

"I love him."

"You've got some balls," drawled Linda letting out a long sigh and leaning back in her chair, "I never dreamed he'd walk in with a cop. I've seen off enough gold diggers. Your folks have got money - but you took your own path. Let's say you've got my respect Anna."

She could have kissed the woman. She wanted to leap up and hug her.

"Okay - my name is Linda - we can work things out."

Anna nodded her agreement as this amazing tough woman carried on talking.

"Let's start with me aged nineteen, pregnant by some French romantic with just a dream of a body who thinks one line of poetry is worth more than all the dollars in the universe. Now there's a bit of that guy in Freddie... he's read more books than there are books.

So one day I can't take any more rabbit stew and cycle rides in the woods. I get a job back in the USA and end up on a trailer park in Castroville with a ten year old kid and a Business degree from the Sorbonne."

"And your folks?"

"They gave up everything to get me to France because that's what I demanded. I know I let them down. They weren't wealthy."

"And Mathieu - Freddie's father?"

Linda tightened her lips in a faint wistful grin.

"We never divorced. There's been no one else. I love him - but I love a lot of other things too. Hey - he's some kinda great poet these days. He must have made at least five hundred dollars by now!" Linda laughed and continued, "Look - I've made choices. I don't dress things up. I like money and security. He was a one off guy you know... crazy but they broke the mould after they made him. We needed two worlds to live in - with a four poster bed in the middle!"

"I respect your openness with me," said Anna.

"Then we respect each other."

Linda stood up and walked to a bureau and took out a photograph album.

"That's the soft stuff Anna - I could talk all day about how I played the markets once Freddie made a bit of cash. But it's not just about that. It's time for you to know the real truth."

She watched as the older woman seemed to sadden and almost wither at what lay ahead.

"This is something I – we - don't talk about. Something at the heart of this whole affair. Everything - absolutely everything is on this fight. I'm going to explain but you must promise that when you leave here today you will just stay clear until it is over. You must promise. I assure you this is not just about me or Freddie. It is about more than you can imagine. Everything up until now has been a sham and you have been just a small part of it. "

Linda fixed her with a pleading stare. How should she respond?

"And after the fight?"

"Then..." Linda paused, visibly chewing her bottom lip, "Then the world is for poetry and lovers. That is my hope Anna."

What choice did she have? Linda might be laying a trail just to distract her but she had to trust her. Once she gave her word she could not go back. She watched as Linda walked to a bookcase and took out a leather bound album.

"I agree Linda - I'll do as you wish."

"Did Freddie ever talk to you about being a kid?"

"He has... but there's been a block there you know. He's talked about fishing and a kid called Ramon he knew on the trailer park."

Linda opened the album and handed it to her. Her eyes picked out a photo of Freddie - maybe sixteen or so with his arm around an Hispanic boy. They both wore boxing gloves, shorts and boots.

"Freddie came to America as a weird little kid speaking three parts French to one part English. He used to read Voltaire and cry for his dad to take him out in the fields. He sure wasn't Yankee Doodle Dandy. So there was this kid - Ramon Gomez. His folks broke their backs on the artichoke fields or any sort of work they could get. The boys were the same age..."

A bell started to ring in Anna's head. She knew that name... something she had seen. Then it came to her.

"The Ramon Gomez Medical Foundation? It's so famous and has some crazy unknown millionaire to bank roll it."

Linda's eyes filled with tears. Anna watched her fighting back emotions that were just too strong for her to contain. Suddenly the dam burst and she buried her face in her hands and sobbed. Uncertain of her reception she crossed the room and put an arm around her.

"I'm sorry Anna... this is just so hard... they were great friends.

All the Gomez boys were boxers and Ramon was a tough boy. Freddie had a lot to learn but soon other kids learned not to mock Freddie for his accent or his books."

Seemingly she had regained her composure and walked to the window looking out over the sea. She carried on with her back to the room, hiding her tears.

"They were both local champions. Ramon got the chance of a pro fight and boy he was training so hard. To be honest he had more guts than speed. One day his sparring partner doesn't show and Freddie's in the gym. The trainer asks him to stand in - but you know - this sparring can be brutal. Freddie plays along and he is so much faster and skilful. The trainer starts bawling and yelling at Ramon - calling him a pussy and macho big guy stuff - you know how it is."

"I know..." agreed Anna with a slight smile.

"In the end Ramon throws the big shot - a real haymaker and Freddie's gets a bloody nose. In the blink of an eye Freddie fires back a left hook - just - KAPOW - a reflex without any thought."

Once again Linda stumbled but did not turn away from the window.

Anna waited in the awful stillness of another woman's grief.

"He died in the hospital of a brain injury. You can't fix up nerve cells. He was nineteen Anna. Dead! Dead! Dead!"

Anna shared the awful sense of unalterable finality that was clearly breaking her heart. Her thoughts flew not to the dead boy but to Freddie. Maybe she should have hidden the deep selfishness in her automatic response.

"Poor Freddie - that poor man. He carries that with him - God I've seen it in his eyes but I had no idea."

Linda turned with unashamed tears rolling down her cheeks as Anna felt the sting of her own tears. In that instant all the stupid barriers between two human beings were breached.

"And the Foundation?" Anna prompted.

"Freddie said he would never box again. Ramon had died of brain damage. No one blamed him but he was a different boy. Then one day he has an idea. All his life he wanted his father to be proud of him. He flew to France and came back with a plan to set up a foundation to study brain and spinal injuries. To fund it he returned to the ring and fought his way up to World Champion. I have managed the business side of things but the Foundation and its achievements are down Freddie."

"He has never said a word of this. No one on this Earth knows this!" Anna gasped astonished, aware from the steady fix of Linda's eyes that there was even more to tell.

"Although he boxed again he swore he would never throw the big punch that had made him a killer. Sadly, the big box office take is for the sluggers - the guys who stand in victory as the loser is writhing and twitching on the floor."

"So he has done it all by skill... surely that's not a problem."

"Not until the mobsters spot that he never goes for the kill and is looking to win on points. If they can fix the referee or the judges or both, the points can go astray."

"So why this fight - he didn't need to take it."

"A few months ago one of the scientists at the Foundation came up with a discovery concerning the cloning of stem cells. There is a real hope now that one day spinal and brain injuries can be treated with new cells. It's early days but the research is expensive and intensive... It's simply a case of making a cool twenty million dollars."

"So Freddie has to fight for the biggest prize he can get. But Linda - he hasn't trained for the fight - they say Brennan will maul him and the referee will let it happen," she exclaimed.

Linda nodded slowly as if making a final decision on going any further.

"Honey - I know it's a cliché but you really can't believe what you read in the papers. Journalists love an easy juicy story - particularly when I feed them one!"

And now she smiled easily and appeared more relaxed. She continued,"he trained here. He hid up and trained for two months in the basement of this house. He trained like no boxer has ever trained. Did he look out of shape to you? Did he ever take off his shirt in public, even on that boat? Believe me - he's in the best shape of his life! He's coming into this fight at 200 pounds and that's solid muscle baby."

"But he wasn't training in London when I met him."

"Oh yes he was - he had done all the hard work. A rest period was needed to build him up a little. I guess he's done a few press ups Anna!" said Linda with a knowing wink.

Anna almost blushed. She did not intend to get drawn down this road.

"So we get to the real business. He had to sign a contract for the fight so he came across to London. I tipped off the paparazzi that he'd be at his restaurant. I suggested he had a girl on his arm..."

"What!" gushed Anna, "What?"

"It's Okay - it doesn't mean he couldn't fall for you - who knows?"

"I guess not... but why?"

"He wanted to back himself to win. The only way he could get the odds where he wanted them was to play at being a slob just looking for a good life and a last pay day. We've put everything on the fight Anna. I mean everything."

"And the likes of Scappaticci and Tondelli - where do they come in?"

Linda smiled.

"We've used them too. Freddie's played along. They'll pay him ten million if he loses. The more money goes on Brennan the better the odds for Freddie. But make no mistake Anna. Boxing is a tough merciless game. When he gets in that ring he's alone and he has to get it right. The word risk doesn't begin to cover it. We can hope but nothing is certain."

Anna sat back and let out a long breath. Everything was clear. He had picked her up in the street because he needed a girl on his arm to please the photographers. He had flaunted her across airports and restaurants. She had come this far to find that she had just been a pawn in a big game. And yet when he had kissed her a few hours ago...

"I'm grateful Linda - it's better that I know."

"There's just a final point. He's in the open now. There'll be spies in the gym reporting back on his shape. These guys can judge a boxer's form by his smell and the look in his eye. To be crude it's like looking over a fence at a bull. Right now Freddie's pawing at the ground and bellowing cos he's just kicked over a hornet's nest. They'll be buzzing baby - and you could get stung. You've agreed not to see him so if you take my advice you'll get back to London while you still can."

She had a point. She pushed aside her fears for herself.

"He just used me Linda - he never loved me did he?"

"Anna - if he said he loved you - then he did."

She searched in Linda's eyes for a measure of her sincerity. There were just too many conflicts to think through. He'd given her a ring, he'd asked her to marry him, they had made fantastic love. She had copied his mobile phone and lied to him about everything in her life.

What was for real? How could she ever know? She loved him beyond her own life but who could believe anything anymore?

She held herself together and stood up to go. Spontaneously Linda came to her and hugged her warmly.

"You'll keep your promise?" she asked searching Anna's eyes for assurance.

"I gave you my word and you have trusted me - that is enough," she replied, holding back her tears until at last she made it back to her car.

She sped away carelessly with her vision blurred, luckily swerving around a U haul removal truck parked opposite the house. One day she would move away from Kilburn. More than likely it would be alone.

Chapter 29

She needed to think calmly. She pulled into the hotel car park and called guardian agent Mayer.

"What's up?" he asked in his uninterested voice. She guessed he was fed up with some stupid English detective running around with nothing to report.

"Big zero - I'm just back at the hotel."

From the corner of her eye she caught a glimpse of a car - the same old Camaro she had seen cruising near the gym in Seaside. The driver was a woman! She relaxed.

"Hey Anna - do you know how many rounds the fight will go?"

"What?"

"You can get real money by betting on the winner and the round. Has Freddie told you anything?"

"No - I can't believe he would know it."

"Just a thought ma'am... if you do get a whisper..."

"Sure."

The Camaro rumbled away. Now a chance to think. She summoned up the memory of his kiss, the look in his deep brown eyes. Could everything have been a fake?

She stepped from the car. The shock of a hand over her mouth, the sickly chemical taste of a cloth and a sensation of slipping into darkness was all she could recall.

"Freddie!" she seemed to scream into the blackness.

Chapter 30

Freddie heard his mother go to the door. He had trained hard but his mind churned with thoughts of Anna. His mother had told her everything but he needed to see her himself. Had she just walked away alone thinking he didn't love her?

The thought was just too much to bear. He had wanted to tell her - tell her that she had originally been just a girl on his arm for a couple of set up photo-shoots. Once things had started to roll and he had fallen so heavily in love with her he could not risk losing her. She must have felt the same about her secret. Poor Anna - poor beautiful baby! He buried his face in his hands trying to blot out his desire and tenderness for her. One day he would have told her about the Foundation and that he was... that he was a killer.

He looked up to see a solid looking guy standing with his mother.

"They got Anna," she said.

Freddie felt adrenalin pumping into his blood. Anger surged through him as he stood up.

"I'm Special Agent John Mayer of the FBI."

"How the hell did this happen?"

"It's Okay Sir - we know where she is. She's in good shape."

"This sounds crazy."

"Let the guy explain," urged Linda.

John Mayer sat down. Freddie assessed him. He looked tough but not too full of it.

"We had her under surveillance. She thought she was just floating around but the whole thing was staked out."

"Why... what? She's just a beautiful girl. They could hurt her. They could rape her," he stammered angrily.

"Everything is being monitored Sir. You haven't seen her police file - she's beautiful but believe me she's got some balls."

Freddie nodded.

"So what's the plan? Where is she?"

"In a rented bungalow in Carmel. The place is bugged and there's a team ready to go in."

"Are you telling me you simply stood back and let it happen?" Freddie raged.

"Not exactly Sir... Do you recall meeting Anna on the jogging path this morning?"

"Sure."

"Did you see a big black guy on skates?"

"I've been seeing him every day... We kinda got to nod at each other."

"He's an agent Sir - there's been a whole team."

"So Anna thinks she's been abducted and that she's on her own. She must be terrified." Linda commented with a waspish edge.

"I agree Ma'am. I flew to London and met with the boss last week - some old bird called Christine Jones. She's one ruthless woman. She knew that Freddie and Anna were kinda close - you know Ma'am - very close. She spotted a newspaper picture and decided to let it run. She wants to get the job done at any cost."

Freddie shook his head. He thought of her in the hands of Tondelli. His skin crawled.

"So they knew she was in too deep and decided to throw her away if it came to it?" he stormed.

"They wanted the best possible evidence... police work has risks Sir,"

"Well, let's go and get her out of there. I'll get my clothes," Freddie leapt up, flexing his shoulders.

"Sir... it's not quite so simple,"

Freddie's cell phone started to ring. He glanced at Mayer.

"Play dumb. Agree to everything... we're recording the call."

With a hard look he answered. "Yo!"

"You're a bad boy Freddie... we've got a deal..."

"Tondelli - what the hell?"

"We're looking after your little beauty. She seemed so alone at that hotel. I'd put her on... but she's kinda... tied up..."

Freddie's blood boiled. He could imagine Tondelli's sneering face.

Agent Mayer made a "down-boy" gesture with his hands.

He knew he had to stay calm.

"What d'ya want?"

"We hear you're in top shape... we're happy for you. We'd back you to win but the odds have collapsed. The word is out that you've been playing a game."

"We've got a deal."

"Sure... we trust you Freddie... but since we're friends we'd just like to hang on to this lovely little girl - just to make sure."

"Where is she - I want to see her."

The line went dead.

"Call Anna's cell phone. If you genuinely knew nothing that is what you would do," ordered Mayer.

Freddie punched her number. It rang...

"How did I know you would call so soon?" rasped Tondelli with a laugh.

"If you hurt her..,"

"We'll be in touch Freddie... don't you go worrying now - you got a big fight coming up,"

"Tondelli!"

He threw down to phone on the sofa as Tondelli hung up, slamming a huge fist into the palm of his hand.

"Let's go... Take me along and you'll get a tip that'll change your life," he yelled at Mayer.

The FBI agent appeared to be thinking.

"It's very irregular Sir. I can swing it just so long as you don't start anything. You'll have my career and pension in your hands. Bring your cell phone. I'll need you to answer if they call."

"Will you stop all this Sir stuff! What do you weigh John - 230 pounds? You look in shape. You and me - we're a team," he declared, pulling off his bath robe and grabbing a pair of jeans to cover his nakedness. Linda averted her eyes. He was not going to accept any arguments.

Two uniformed cops strolled in.

"We're taking care of your Mom," explained Mayer.

Chapter 31

She felt sick. A light was filtering through closed curtains. She could hear voices in another room. A cell phone rang with the same ring tone as her own. Her mouth was filled with a cloth and her lips taped. Her hands were numb and tied behind her. It felt like she was on a mattress. In the dim light she looked down to see that her ankles were tied with thick blue tape.

She began to analyze her situation. She had been grabbed outside the hotel. Some form of chloroform type chemical had been used to sedate her. Vaguely she remembered a journey on the floor of a van and being carried through the garage and kitchen of a house. She had not come far - no more than five or six miles. The room smelled dusty and damp.

She heard a movement and heard footsteps. A figure stood above her.

"If you yell I'll tape you back up," said a voice she recognized.

A large hand ripped more blue tape from her lips and pulled the cloth from her mouth. He threw it in the corner. She noted the place. Fingerprints, DNA. She had to be professional.

"We just gotta stop meeting like this," she spat at the ugly form of Tondelli.

"Your man's a bad boy my little English Rose. We're only making sure he understands how much we care about our business."

"What the hell can I do?"

"Just be beautiful baby... he'll be longing for loving company."

He squatted down and pulled her upright. He pulled out an evil knife and cut the tapes on her wrists. She felt an agony as the blood surged back into her arms and hands.

He smiled, letting the point of the blade trace up her leg to her groin.

"Sweet meat aren't you?" he whispered hoarsely.

She stared at his large pock marked face, his loose flabby lips and stained carnivorous teeth.

"You wouldn't dare," she threw at him.

"Just be a good little girl..."

She noted that the outside light was beginning to fade. In the morning Agent Mayer would come to the hotel if she did not call in. In another room she caught two different voices. She studied the bay window. It had single flimsy glazing. She ran through her favorite Metropolitan Police issue karate chop with the side of her hand up under the nose. When her chance came it would have to connect. A chance would come.

Tondelli clicked on a light and slumped down in an armchair. She saw her handbag on the floor and watched him pick it up. No worries. No warrant card, no police ID. He pulled out a tube ticket and read it. It was going to be a long night.

Chapter 32

John Mayer drove sedately out to Carmel. Freddie sat alongside containing his impatience and anger.

"She's gonna be fine," said the agent. "she's been in some spots I can tell you," Freddie relaxed a little.

"You know John - it seems amazing. I simply met a wonderful girl - I had no idea. Those beautiful eyes - her silky skin - that long black hair - a cop? I still can't believe it."

"You don't really seem too much like my idea of a boxer."

"I guess not."

"Can I ask you a personal question Freddie?"

"Sure."

"What round will you win the fight?"

"If we get her out and she's not hurt I'll tell you exactly what's going to happen. If you listen to what I tell you and trust me you won't have to worry too much about your pension one way or the other."

Agent Mayer smiled and drove on. A few minutes later they pulled up behind a U haul truck in a small car park surrounded by trees. An old Camaro was parked alongside. They scrambled into the truck. The huge black skater guy was wearing earphones. Two other agents shifted to make room.

"Meet the team."

Freddie shook hands all round.

"You guys are amazing... I'll never just pass anyone in the street again."

"The house is about 150 yards away to the left. We're listening to every word. She's on a mattress on the floor in the front room. Tondelli's there but things are fairly loose. They're not expecting anything. They've moved her car to a lonely beach. Just another story of a missing girl, maybe walked into the sea with a broken heart. The driver's been pulled over by the Highway Patrol. He's already started to talk. The thug who was following to pick him up is in the morgue. What they call an exchange of fire. These guys are going away Freddie!"

"The morgue - what the hell are we doing letting them keep her?"

His thoughts churned with the loveliness of her - in the hands of killers.

He remembered her last kiss as she had met him on the path that morning. He wanted her for a lifetime and maybe now there could never be even another touch - another moment.

"What's happening in there?" he snapped.

"Nothing - sounds like he's looking through some stuff - maybe her bag," drawled the ex-skater.

Mayer seemed relaxed.

"There won't be any police ID. She's a pro - we'll go in at Four o'clock. That's when the body slows down. That's when the truck driver's fall off the road and the junkies die."

Freddie reflected. These guys were from a different world. This was Anna's life too - where the terrible and the obscene was just a line of casual conversation. When all this was over could she be the woman he had met and fallen in love with at first sight?

Now he understood some of the things she had said - about the poor and the sorrow of things. Behind her mask she had to be a different woman, just so much more of a woman than he could ever have imagined. Now she lay tied up while a killer stood over her. She could have stayed safe back in London. He was unworthy of her love. He had been so heartless and cruel on that boat when he had stormed off. He could see the love in her eyes and yet his pride overwhelmed him because she had fooled him. No one got the better of Freddie La Salle even though he could feel her soft true love for him in every touch. Still he had not backed down and called her or taken her in his arms. Once before his pride had snapped a response and his friend lay dead. He had learned nothing.

He surveyed the agents calmly waiting to raid the house. The skater appeared to tense a little and press the earphones more closely. He flicked a switch and a speaker came on. It was the voice of Mauro Tondelli.

Chapter 33

She watched as Tondelli examined a business card. Her heart raced. Her palms sweated. Her feet were still tied but her arms were free and had come back to life. This was trouble. She watched as he tried to read the small writing. She had been careless and it could cost her dear. She saw his lips attempting to spell out the unfamiliar words. Christine Jones - Deputy Assistant Commissioner, New Scotland Yard.

He looked at her with a quizzical expression, appearing not to understand the possibilities immediately.

"New Scotland Yard... that's limey police... Sherlock Holmes and that guy Watson."

"Sherlock Holmes was a private detective," Anna informed him, hoping to appear untroubled. Tondelli gazed at her and turned the card over and over in his fat hands.

"I'm thinking you're a cop..." he snarled.

"Cop! Do I look like a cop?" she laughed, remembering only too well when she had last spoken those words.

The joke was not lost on Freddie. She had said the same thing in the London taxi a few minutes after they had met.

Mayer spoke into a police radio.

"All units stand-by," he glanced at the skater, "they're still in that front room,"

"Go! Go! Go!" yelled Mayer, springing from the truck.

Freddie followed, ignoring his pleas to hold back. He thought of nothing but her - his lover - his woman.

Agents were running at the bungalow. A team was at the porch door with a battering ram. Freddie saw the front window with a light behind. The bulk of a standing male figure was his target. The glass looked old and thin. His hooded top was thick. He pulled it up to cover his head and built up speed. He drew his forearms up over his face and played one final flashback of her face across his consciousness before he took off and waited for the crash.

Chapter 34

"You bitch!" exclaimed Tondelli, clenching the muscles in his cheek as a rage of realization swept over him, "you're gonna start explaining..."

He pulled out the knife and stared at her breasts. She squirmed, guessing that some kind of favorite torture was about to commence.

"You don't need the knife.." she began.

She heard a stun grenade in the back room and a commotion at the front door. Tondelli remained transfixed.

A terrific crash smashed the window to fragments of flying glass. Some guy in a hooded top and jeans hurtled in to the room like a canon ball and rolled to absorb the impact. She just had the time to scrabble aside. Tondelli fumbled in his jacket. She saw the handle of a firearm. In a split second the hooded guy fired a punch so hard that Tondelli's nose was replaced by a squelch of blood.

Anna grabbed the knife and cut the tape around her ankles. Tondelli gurgled on the floor holding his hands to his face. The door flew open and Agent Mayer bustled in holding some other guy in a headlock.

"Freddie - you promised to stay out of this!" he gasped.

"And I promised you some of the best advice you'll ever get..."

Anna's senses swam. Freddie? Did he say Freddie?

The guy was brushing himself off and had his back to her. Another agent rushed in and cuffed Tondelli. Then he calmly stowed the gun and the knife in evidence bags. Anna stared at him in amazement.

"You had a bandana. You drive a Camaro..."

The agent smiled. Everything was becoming clear. The FBI had expected this. She had been under surveillance. Mayer's indifference had been a front. But just who was the guy who had arrived via the window? That was not a police technique and the punch...

Then she saw him. A wide smile lit up his face as his dark eyes burned with love. She saw the massive width of his shoulders and the rock hard bulk of his thighs in his tight faded blue jeans.

"Freddie! How can you be here?" she shrieked in disbelief.

"I got friends."

Agent Mayer snorted, "We don't encourage citizens to leap through windows."

"I'm not a citizen John - I'm a Frog. That's how come I can jump. Anyhow when you write this up I was never here. The fat guy on the floor won't remember much."

Both Anna and Mayer laughed as Freddie drew her into his arms and kissed her. She felt the solid strength of his body and the softness of his lips and knew deep down that she was loved.

"Guys... I'd love to let everyone go but..." began Agent Mayer.

"But there's paperwork right?" added Anna with a smile.

"Different continent - same crap..."

She snuggled into him as they walked back down the driveway. Never had she felt so safe and protected. She smiled as she spotted the skater and the female jogger in the car park. Hadn't she nearly driven into a U Haul truck outside Linda's house?

She squeezed into Mayer's car. Freddie stayed outside and put his arm around the agent's shoulder and walked him away from the car. She heard the beginning of what was said.

"John - you know in this life that things can't always work out. No one else will know this but this is the way I'm seeing it..."

She watched them move away and saw Freddie demonstrate a couple of punches. The agent nodded seriously. They began to walk back. She caught Freddie's final words.

"If it doesn't work out - there is no plan B. It has to work!"

Both men slid into the car and rolled down to the Monterey Police Station in Madison Street. So much for the action. Now for the grind of police procedure. At least no one expected her to know all the form numbers.

Chapter 35

It was dawn as they tumbled into the back of a police cruiser for the ride back to the hotel.

"Can you guys drop us at the wharf?" said Freddie suddenly.

The cop shrugged and pulled over. It had been a long night. The world was still quiet, hovering on the brink of a new day and new beginnings. She felt his strong arm around her as they strolled onto the boardwalk. The creak of boats at their moorings and the calm lub-dub of the swell around the pier soothed her like a lullaby. There was so much to say - so much to explain.

He seemed to have read her thoughts and smiled down at her.

"I thought back in London that at last my life had truly begun - that the past was the past. Perhaps we should start today."

"Love starts every day Freddie - how many days can we start again?" she asked staring up into his face. Once again she reached up to touch the scar over his beautiful eye.

Her eyes misted with tears, focusing once more on what still lay ahead of him. He was gambling everything for the sake of the Foundation. He softly brushed her cheek with the back of his fingers.

"I am Champion of the world you know. I'm gonna make it."

"But I heard you tell Agent Mayer that there was no plan B."

"No one who ever won much had a plan B Honey! You were the plan A of my dreams since I had dreams. I kept dreaming you up until you were real. It was a rocky old road - if you still want me - even if I wind up with nothing."

She threw her arms around his neck and kissed him as he picked her up and cradled her as if she were weightless. She felt the force of his knotted steel body and the rasp of his stubble as he kissed her again. She closed her eyes and let herself melt into him, losing the boundaries between her being and his.

"It's not enough to say I love you Anna - it seems too little - such pale little words."

"Like the pale light of dawn - like a new day," she whispered.

"Maybe love is just the beginning of what a man and a woman are to each other - like a bud promising a flower," he replied in a deep slow voice.

The warmth of his body seeped into her as he held her tirelessly in his arms. Now that all the drama had passed, her mind rolled idly to her belly. There had been so many things to think about. She too had gone for broke… there was no plan B and Nature held the plan A. Soon enough she would get a clue...

The distant throb of a fishing boat nosing out into the swell, the sound of a radio belting out the latest hit on the breakfast show, a line of pelicans in echelon sweeping along the shore announced the unstoppable rise of the sun. Sea lions barked, blinked and preened their whiskers for the tourists. It was a routine day for the teeming life in Monterey Bay. Several prisoners prepared for their moment in court. Two lovers strolled hand in hand down Cannery Row to the Monterey Bay Inn.

He lay back on the bed watching her. He was tired and yet her beauty enlivened and excited him. Her richly dark hair cascaded down her back. Her deep gray blue eyes were soft and loving. He stood and stripped off - aware of her eyes on him. All he wore was a jogging top and jeans with worn out trainers that he had grabbed as he had left the house.

Wordlessly they shared the shower, laughing as they soaped each other's bodies, both aware that things could have ended very differently.

He felt the joy of her breasts as his hands soothed across her nipples. The act aroused him. She giggled and let her hand stroke down across the rippled six pack of his stomach until he jolted with a deep grunt as she touched the spot. He wanted her - but not in urgency - not as a release. He enjoyed the tension of his desire for her. This was something he had never felt for any woman until now. Her soft breasts, her womb were his opposite and by contrast defined the hardness of him. Yet it was also his origin - the place where he had found life and succor. Suddenly he knew the secrets of the ancient priestess - how this well of life had drawn men to worship its beauty. For now he did not want to break the spell of her loveliness. One day his child would grow from her gentle strength and he could do no more than offer the pulse of his life to the vessel of her promise.

He toweled her body tenderly and returned to the bed where they knelt facing each other. The Cartier diamond still sparkled on its chain between her breasts. He unhooked the clasp and held the ring.

"Few men get the chance to live their happiest moment twice," he smiled, slipping the platinum band back onto her finger. Her lips called him to kiss her as they lay back and entwined in the warmth of a deep love that was beyond the physical joy of sex.

She felt the growing tension of her body. His head lay on the pillow, angled down to draw her nipple into his mouth. His hand stroked tenderly between her thighs as her juices responded to his growing need for her.

In a gentle choreography of mutual longing he moved inside her and softly they abandoned their own selves into a single point of ecstasy.

Too soon, too soon the turning world out-roared the peace of lovers and he rose to go. She knew that this would be the last time she would really see him until it was over. She watched him move around the room. Her tears fell softly. Perhaps the lovers of gladiators in ancient Rome had known such partings. Perhaps they had felt the same awful sorrow mixed with pride. His lips came to hers for one last time and he was gone. For now she would live as a mask hiding an empty shell. Her life was gone. Her man had taken it and held it in no more and no less than his fist.

Chapter 36

The days were a blur. She shopped with Linda, choosing and un-choosing fight night outfits. She posed for photos, talked to Time magazine and National Enquirer. She went to the Monterey police department for a video conference with Christine Jones. It had been a brief release from the tension. Christine was to be Baroness Jones of Streatham - the place where she had once been the Blue Witch. The tough old girl deserved her celebrity and her place in the sun. What had she known of love? What ache was in her soul? Was it that same ache that had dulled all her joys until she had met Freddie?

The American Airlines staff on the New York flight out of San Francisco poured champagne and asked for signed photos of Freddie that Linda carried in her executive briefcase. To her it was business. Routine!

They conspired not to talk of the fight yet Anna thought of nothing else. She heard the braying mob chanting for Brennan to attack. She re-ran all those magazine shots of fighters with their swollen faces pouring blood. A few times Linda reached for her in a silent hug or the squeeze of her hand.

"Just think of all those wives, mothers and sweethearts with loved ones away in the military Honey. They've got no wealth or fame," she said plainly.

The yellow cabs and the manic streets of New York seemed unreal. The Park-View suite at the Ritz Carlton on Central Park South offered unbelievable opulence and splendor. Liveried drivers of horse drawn carriages awaited custom. She toured the park in an open landau with Linda and yet she could have been anywhere, could have been anyone, could have eaten caviar or a hot dog and not known the difference. They stayed away from him. Linda said time and time again that he was in a zone where no one except his trainer and a couple of corner men could follow. The papers showed a picture from the weigh-in. Brennan was ugly and pointing, making threats and pumping himself up. Freddie looked calm and deadly serious. The whole show was hyped as the home town hero against the foreign Frenchman. Often Linda chuckled since a lot of the copy was planted by her.

Chapter 37

The day came. A limo collected them from the hotel and took the slow prowl to Madison Square Garden. The show had already started with a bill of lesser fights. The main event was scheduled for nine o'clock when the guys had their beer and had watched the car commercials. She had dressed in a red silk knee length wrap over dress with killer heels and a black double breasted wool coat.

A riot of photographers snapped at all the arriving limos. A few called her name. She had become a bit of a celebrity in her own right. The chat show offers rolled in. In any other life it would have been wonderful. But not in her life. She lived through a lump in her throat and the ever present prick of tears behind her eyes. Perhaps she was not made to love? Perhaps she loved too much? She longed to be with him. She knew she could not.

A mob of security guys led them through a maze of corridors. At last they reached a crowd of big men in evening suits who all looked like boxers. Seeing the two women they edged aside until Anna found herself at a dressing room door guarded by no one other than Agent John Mayer.

"He's asked to see you Anna," he shouted above the hubbub. She glanced questioningly at Linda.

"At this point he's the boss. You've only got a couple of minutes."

She entered the room, surprised by the calm silence. He was sitting on a treatment table gloved up and wrapped in his ring gown. She could tell he was focused. A coil of passion, pride and anger was set in his face. He knew what he had to do. He knew what was at stake. She wanted to talk of love but nothing must soften him now. She longed to rest a tender hand on his face.

"Show me your finger," he said firmly.

She held out her hand, displaying the sparkling diamond ring. He nodded approval.

"You are mine Anna. In a few minutes our lives together can begin. I must do something that my soul rebels against. You are my strength."

She held back her urge to go to him. Suddenly the room filled with men and he was swept away, shadow boxing and bouncing his way to the ring.

"Aren't you going ringside?" asked John Mayer, joining her on the treatment table.

"I couldn't..."

"Me neither,"

"Did you place a bet?"

"Just about everything and a bit more Anna. I believe in that guy."

She was too numb to respond.

He jumped up and switched on a TV set on the wall. Two commentators were talking excitedly. Her heart raced. Her mouth was dry. She glanced at the screen. The fighters were in the middle of the ring. She heard the referee.

"I wanna clean fight. Break when I say break. Touch gloves and come out fighting."

A bell rang. A crowd of one hundred thousand yelled. She could not bear to watch but the commentary continued uninvited.

"La Salle looks in great shape - he comes straight to the center of the ring - he'll be looking for a steady start - Brennan's looking to come straight inside - La Salle stands his ground - this is unusual - he pushes Brennan back and follows it with a sharp jab to the body - Brennan doesn't like that - he rushes in but La Salle keeps the center of the ring. Brennan's gonna have to soak up some jabs to get in close. La Salle drops his gloves and dances away, teasing the New York boy. This is not the regular La Salle folks - this guy is not a puncher - this is gonna be interesting!"

The commentator's voice rose to a shout. The crowd bayed like one huge beast.

"Brennan rushes in, La Salle jabs but Brennan dips his shoulder and throws a right cross. La Salle's head snaps back - he's hurt but on his feet. Brennan storms in for the kill - he thinks he's got him - this is sensational folks! La Salle seems dazed, he leads out with a straight right hand but has no power - Brennan sets himself up for the big one!"

Anna flicked her eyes up to the screen. She could see blood on Freddie's mouth. The crowd was screaming "Bih-lee Bih-lee".The commentator reached new heights -

"La Salle bounces again - he drops his gloves taunting the challenger - Brennan needs to keep his cool here - La Salle is not champion of the world for nothing. He's taken Brennan's best shot and he's back on his toes. Brennan tries to come inside - throws the right cross again- misses by a mile - he's off balance- - La Salle throws a vicious left hook! What a punch! Oh my Lord - what a punch. Brennan is on the floor! He's not moving - The referee pushes La Salle away - the medics are rushing in to the ring. It's over Ladies and Gentleman... the fight is over."

The screen showed Brennan slowly starting to move. Action replays of the punch turned in slow motion. Anna watched in disbelief. The punch had hit Brennan like a train. So this was the knockout punch that had killed Ramon Gomez - the punch that he could never throw. Suddenly she is being spun round by Agent Mayer.

"My kids are going Yale!" he bellowed tears of joy coursing down his face, "I put the house and every cent on him to win by a first round knock - down. I got 40 to 1. It was his only hope - he knew that. The guy's a God."

He pulled her by the arm out in the arena. A giant screen was showing shots of Freddie in Brennan's corner hugging the loser who was back on his feet. The MC bawled out the result while the referee raised Freddie's arm.

"The winner by a knockout and still champion of the world... out of Paris France... Frrrrrreddie... Le Professeur... Laaaaaa... Salle!!!"

A disappointed crowd still cheered in recognition of his awesome power.

Somehow she was swept along and lifted to the ring. Linda was giving an interview. Then she was in his arms. His heat and sweat overwhelmed her.

"That life is over Anna. I have so many plans for us," she reached out and pressed her fingers to a gash on his lip.

"They may have already started," she smiled as his blood trickled onto her fingers.

"I love you Anna," he said with the warmth once again glowing in his dark eyes.

"And I you," she replied.

Epilogue

Madame Anna La Salle watched nervously as her toddler Xavier teetered unsteadily across the uneven flagstones of the champagne vineyard farmhouse. Freddie moved behind her, placing his huge warm hand possessively on her belly, restraining her instinct to rush across in case the boy fell.

"Freddie - he'll fall!"

"And he'll get up," he chuckled warmly.

Inevitably he tumbled and rolled over with a giggle. Freddie went to him and picked him up and sat him high on his shoulders.

"Voila - ta mère needs to relax," he confided to the boy.

"He needs to get cleaned up - your father is arriving," Anna reminded him.

"And Mom too... this is sure some plan of yours."

"They still love each other. He has dedicated his new collection of poems to her. He will be giving her the first copy tonight after dinner."

"Did he tell you that himself?"

"No - but you'll tell him just as soon as he gets here," she said, reaching out to touch his cheek and kiss his lips.

Fin

FREE DOWNLOAD

Meet the Passion Patrol Team

Get this full-length
suspense romance novel

FREE

when you line up with
The Passion Patrol

...Join Emma Calin's
VIP Reader Club

*"Emma Calin has written another
gripping romantic suspense
with plenty of both."*
P. Rees-Rohrbacker

Get My Free Book

Join Emma Calin's VIP Reader Group, keep up to date with forthcoming books, advanced publication offers, giveaways and special promotions and get a free e-copy of '*GUILT*', another Passion Patrol Series novel. Click the link or scan the QR code from your smart device or phone.

http://smarturl.it/VIPPP1

Other titles by Emma Calin:

The Passion Patrol Series Box Set 1

Grab the first three books in the series PLUS the companion cookbook to the second in the series in one **bargain** bundle. Titles included: *Combat, Dynasty, Seduction of Taste* and *Crowns.*

The Passion Patrol Series Box Set 2

Grab the next three books in the series in one **bargain** bundle. Titles included: *Santa, Wealth* and *Guilt.*

Dynasty

A sexy aristocrat. A wild-child inner city cop. A crime wave of passion.

A steamy romance novel introducing a sassy female police officer who locks up criminals and always gets her man.

Moved out from the city after one-too-many maverick missions, Shannon discovers there's more going on in the sleepy country village than meets the eye. The son of a local aristocrat arouses suspicion of drug crime activity... but his widower father arouses more animal instincts!

Could she really mix with the British Royal Family? Can she risk her heart and career on yet another high-risk unauthorized investigation? Can she get justice for an innocent boy? Dare a kid from the gutter dream of being a countess?

Wild child inner city cop Shannon Aguerri walks a dangerous line between her methods and justice. When the bosses lose their nerve, she is transferred to green pastures to play out the role of a routine village cop. In Fleetworth-Green she encounters signs of people and drug trafficking and homes-in on serious millionaire criminals. As a loner she has attracted men but nothing has stuck. When she meets Spencer, the hunky and widowed Earl of Bloxington, there is an immediate rapport between them. Their social differences mean nothing to their passion and need. Already in the mix is an upper-class female rival who has long plotted her way into the earl's bed. The jealousy is an evil shade of green and the anger is a violent scarlet.

Often inhibited by a sense of duty and honor, Spencer is slow to reveal his feelings. When Shannon confronts him with the need to choose between her word and that of her rival, he does not immediately support her. All the same, when they are forced together to carry out a desperate rescue mission, their love is stronger than everything ranged against them.

Please note: This book contains joyful sex between adults in a consenting relationship. There is also strong language in high-stress police confrontations with criminals.

Santa

Another Passion Patrol novel from Emma Calin. This time with a holiday twist. I wonder what this naughty Santa has in his sack for our intrepid cop?

Crowns

Introducing street cop Sophia Castellana who gets drawn into a world of international political intrigue, crime, romance and adventure, after rescuing a young pop idol from a violent attempted kidnapping—and who demands to have Sophia as his private bodyguard…and more.

Seduction of Taste

Hot Cops. Hot Crime. Hot Romance..... Hot Food?

Seduction of Taste is the companion cookbook to the hot romance novel, *Dynasty*.

A total of thirty-one recipes from appetizers and main courses to suggestions for sandwich fillings at a traditional afternoon tea. Late night suppers and romantic meals for two. Food is the music of love. It sets the tone and the pace. It provides those moments when tastes and textures shared at the table form a metaphor for the physical appetites of love and lust.

Read the romance, feel the passion, taste the love!

Wealth

What would you do if your bosses told you to break the law? How far would you go before you questioned them? What if you're a cop and your bosses are the law?

City cop Kaitlyn Thorn must keep enigmatic banker Randolf Quinn alive at all costs. Betrayed and on the run from her team she must gamble on nothing but her own instincts.

Can she trust their love and save them both from destruction?

Guilt

Gunfire....

...A police dog is down.

Lonely dog handler Helen carries the guilt of survivor. Star singer and single father Marco is too guilty to sing.
Both are too guilty to love.
They meet as an innocent animal fights for life. *Perhaps a hope is born?*
Terror fanatics close in on London, their target the Queen. A cop must follow her orders. A father must protect his child.
Love breaks laws and hearts.
Follow the lust and drama. Let go of the guilt. Enjoy the thrill of the action. Follow Marco and Helen to the climax of passion. Hold on for the ride to the triumph of love

Coming soon...

Emma Calin's new Passion Patrol Novels:
Power **(Summer 2019)**
Desire **(Autumn 2019)**

Sub-Prime (#1 The Love in a Hopeless Place Collection)

Two powerless beings are swept together in a transient struggle for survival. Could the human spirit transcend the brutality and indifference of their brief experience before they are once again swept helplessly apart? Far more than a love story — this is a story about love

Sub-Prime: a short story of our times.

The Chosen (#2 The Love in a Hopeless Place Collection)

A woman, a man, a van, and a plan. When the luck runs out; the lucky walk away. A short story set in the extremis of everyday.

Escape to Love (#3 The Love in a Hopeless Place Collection)

A woman on the run from domestic violence with no one but her vulnerable autistic teenage child as a companion lives in isolation and fear. While her hand-to-mouth scenarios are played out in the shadow of a threatening suspense, a story of crime and love unfolds around her.

Angela (#4 The Love in a Hopeless Place Collection)

A mystery tale of a late-night taxi ride where the final passenger may not be all that she seems.

Love in a Hopeless Place (#5 The Love in a Hopeless Place Collection)

A mature woman finds the truth of herself. She cannot go back even though physical and emotional violence erupt around her.

Dare she give in to love?

Will sexual passion and fear overwhelm her stable life?

Whom can she trust to love her for herself?

The Love in a Hopeless Place Collection

Emma Calin's complete set of short stories and novelettes, available in one bargain "boxed set." This edition includes *Sub-Prime, The Chosen, Escape To Love, Love In A Hopeless Place* and short story: *Angela.*

Children's Books by Emma Calin:

The "Once Upon a NOW!" Series

The "ONCE UPON A NOW!" books form a series of illustrated, interactive children's stories, in the true fairy tale tradition with modern-day settings. Each is available in paperback, Kindle, and audio book formats. Digital versions come with clickable links to bonus video clips, photos, and drawings to color. The paperback has QR codes to scan and take you to the same bonus material to enrich the stories.

Coming soon… The complete Box Set of all three books in the *"Once Upon a Now Series"* for Kindle.

Alf The Workshop Dog

How could a scruffy dog in a bus depot, and the call of crows link back to another world of power and love?

The ancient Kingdom of Zanubia and a stray dog looking for scraps in an inner-city repair garage, hold the secret. A wicked king, a beautiful girl, a young prince and the struggle between right and wrong maintain the fable tradition.

Isabella's Pink Bicycle

There's something strange in the woodshed....

A poor little girl in a faraway land dreams of riding a pink bicycle. When she meets a strange animal, her dreams come true. Her happiness turns to sadness when a tragedy occurs in the town and her father doesn't come home.

Maybe her new magic friend can find him?

Kool Kid Kruncha and the High Trapeze

Charlie finds it tough when his parents divorce, but Auntie Kate helps him overcome his greatest fear.

When Charlie has to move from the country into the city, he leaves behind his home, his mates, and his beloved football team. He will need to make new friends. With his small size and red hair, some people aren't kind to him. He wonders if he can face another day at school.

A trip to the circus gives him the strength to see himself and others in a new way.

About Emma Calin

Novelist, philosopher, blogger, poet, would be master chef. A woman pedaling between Peckham & Pigalle, in search of passion & enduring romance.

Emma Calin writes romance novels, gritty short stories and children's fiction about love and survival in the 21st century. She has published a number of digital, paperback and audio books which are available from Amazon and other good bookstores worldwide.

She blogs about her dual life in St-Savinien sur Charente in south west France and Romsey, a market town in southern England. She feels extremely lucky to be able to experience the world and life through these two, very different, lenses. She spends any time she can, when not writing, on her tandem exploring the countryside or in her kayak on the River Charente.

Emma also records and produces audio books and plays the trombone (although not at the same time).

Find Emma on the Internet

If you'd like an autograph for any of Emma's books, there is a cool digital service called 'Authograph' where you can say hello and get a personalized signature.

http://www.authorgraph.com/authors/EmmaCalin

Website: **http://www.emmacalin.com**

Blog: **http://emmacalinblog.com/**

Twitter: **http://twitter.com/EmmaCalin**

Facebook: **http://www.facebook.com/emma.calin**

Facebook Fan Page: **http://www.facebook.com/PassionPatrol**

Facebook Fan Page: **http://www.facebook.com/EmmaCalin**

Goodreads:
http://www.goodreads.com/author/show/4915751.Emma_Calin

Amazon Author Page:
http://www.viewAuthor.at/EmmaCalin

Instagram: **@VirtualBookCafe**

A note from Emma Calin

Thank you so much for reading my *'Passion Patrol'* novel, *COMBAT*. I hope you found it entertaining and enjoyable and that you'll go on to read the rest of the series.

I would be so grateful if you would leave a rating on Amazon, or even a review if you have the time - your feedback is invaluable and really helps us Indie Authors in our endless quest for visibility.

Say hello if you are passing on Twitter or Facebook - I try and get back to all mentions and messages within a few days.

Sign up to my mailing list if you'd like regular updates about my new books – you'll get a free e-book as a welcome gift. Here's the link:

http://smarturl.it/VIPPP1 or scan the QR code below:

Thanks again and very best wishes.

Emma x

Publisher

This book was published by Gallo-Romano Media. For details of other books and authors or if you would like to submit your book for publishing:
Email contact@gallo-romano.co.uk